WHISPER ME

∞ ∞

GRACE BRANNIGAN

P.O. Box 100
East Jewett, New York, 12424 USA

Whisper Me

Women of Character Contemporary Series
Echoes From the Past
Once and Always
Heartstealer
Wishing on a Rodeo Moon

Women of Strength Time Travel Series
Once Upon a Remembrance
Soulmates Through Time
Treasure So Rare

Romantic Short Stories
Two Babies, a Cowboy and Sara
Deception

Faeries Lost Series
Find Me
Whisper Me
Hear Me

Website: www.GraceBrannigan.com

All Characters, places and events are fictitious and are not associated or inspired by any person living or dead.

Cover art by Steph's Cover Design

Print Edition Copyright 2015   Elaine Warfield

ISBN: 978-1-939061-47-8

License Notes

∞ Chapter One ∞

LILJA WAVED GOLD FAERIE DUST over the portal, watching Greyson Maddox walk in the lands wedged between the river and the hills of the earth realm. His dark hair was sprinkled with flecks of snow and he was dressed for the bitter cold of the snowy day. Curiously, she observed his expression as he stared up at the sky. She sensed his aloneness and saw clearly the fracture of his soul. It touched her, and she reached her hand through the portal, placing a whisper soft stroke upon his temple, intent on comforting the man she had known since he was a child.

"Lilja!" Her best friend Peripaus quickly grabbed her arm and pulled her back from the portal. "What are you thinking? Are you bewitched?"

Lilja indicated the man. "Peri, look at how sad --"

"You know it is frowned upon to interact with the humans."

"Faeries have been mixing with humans for years," Lilja said, still watching Grey.

"The council discourages those interactions. Our worlds are too divided."

"So they say," Lilja replied, "but truthfully, I have never seen evidence of such division."

"Hush," Peri said, quickly looking around. "Would you question the wisdom of the elders?"

Lilja smiled at her friend, admiring the soft gold braid of her hair as it lay upon one shoulder. "Oh, dear Peri, do not look worried. There are no elders hiding in the ferns." She jumped up and quickly ran around the forest clearing, peering into the bushes, laughing aloud as Peri scolded her for her merriment. Finally, Lilja plopped down on the sun-warmed earth. "There! No elders hiding in the bushes!" she exclaimed and dissolved into laughter.

Peri looked even more alarmed, her deep purple eyes darting this way and that. Then her gaze lifted and she saw the mischief in Lilja's face. Together they began to laugh.

Lilja held out her hand. "Peri, you are so very serious. Come and sit next to me on the ferns."

Together they settled back against the soft, feathery ferns, facing the brilliant blue sky above them. Lilja stretched her arms up to the warmth of the sun. Peace, comfort and joy enveloped them in this perfect little world. Lilja knew the beauty and grandeur of Aisywel was a faerie realm unlike any other and yet ... she sighed. "I find it strange that the humans choose not to see us."

"Some do, you know," said Peri. "The ones with The Sight."

Lilja gave in to another gurgle of laughter. "Peri, they call them psychics now. The Sight is old school."

Peri frowned at her and slapped her lightly on the arm. "Well, you know I cling to the old ways. I shall probably never change."

Lilja smiled at her friend fondly. "And for that I am glad." She gave Peri a playful grin. "Just as I shall not change."

"Well, that is no doubt true. But do be careful in your enthusiasm and fascination with the humans. I hear whispers, you know." She looked out over the meadow, catching sight of a silky black rabbit hopping through the high grass in search of breakfast. Above them scarlet fireflies rested delicately in the tree branches until called upon to light Aisywel at dusk. "I have traveled far and wide among the faerie realms. I hear lots of stories. I prefer the faerie realms over those heavier realms."

Lilja grew a bit pensive. "Don't you find it curious that a race so gifted by life, many times seems at a loss what to do with their emotions? They cause each other distress, give in to excesses, and appear to lose sight of how precious life is."

"You spend too much time watching them," Peri said. "I have a difficult time understanding why."

"Perhaps because I have visited them for many years and I've become comfortable with their ways. I have seen you watching them a time or two," Lilja added teasingly as she rose to her feet. She gathered little bits of faerie dust from the ground around them and placing it in her palm, blew gently over her friend.

Peri grimaced in her serious way. "Lilja, I study them so that I might understand your interest!" she retorted, then she shivered. "I would never want to live with the humans. They are loud, they can't control their anger, and they -- they smell."

Lilja was intrigued. "You curl up your nose -- why would you say they smell?"

Peri was silent a moment, and Lilja coaxed her. "Come, tell me and I will share a secret or two with you."

Peri hesitated then said, "That time I visited the earth plane with Herrikus ..."

Lilja nodded. Peri's previous love interest upon her arrival to Aisywel had been Herrikus, a delicate and extremely pale-skinned faerie. He had not been the right faerie for her friend. Frankly, Lilja had not understood Peri's fascination with the boy. He had broken Peri's heart when he ran off with a faerie from a lower vibration.

"We only popped in for a quick look," Peri said. "But it was right in the middle of a terrible fight between two humans. One of them fell against me." She grimaced and shook her head.

"Well, you can't base all humans on that one experience. Remember that one time you came with me on one of my visits? All those lovely horses and you were intent on painting each and every one --"

"You have to admit the horses were magnificent, more enchanting than any here on Aisywel. So many shades of perfection to capture."

Lilja chuckled. "Shush, now -- you will be making our mystical beasts jealous."

Peri's eyes grew a bit dreamy. "There is just

something spectacular about them, even if they do reside in that dense realm."

"And what of the humans who were working with them?" Lilja asked curiously, thinking of Grey and the vast ranch out in the earth dimension.

Peri's face grew a bit red and she admitted, "I'm always curious about new subjects to paint." She looked over at her. "What secrets do you have to tell?"

"I'd love to study the humans in more detail," Lilja said dreamily, smiling. "If it were entirely of my choosing, I would paint a beautiful color over their pain and take it away so they never felt it."

"Lilja!"

Lilja shrugged. "Men and women take unimaginable risks when under the influence of their emotions. I find that a curious thing."

Lilja moved closer to the portal so that she might see the man again. "When I think of the scent of a human," she nodded at the man, "I think of Grey. He is redolent of hay and the outdoors. Such a sweet scent on a man." She gurgled with laughter. "Even if he is a human."

Peri frowned at her, her concern evident. "Why always this man?" Peri asked quietly. She tilted her head, studying him through the portal. "He is rather handsome," she admitted grudgingly. "He's very tall, though. Taller than the faeries."

Lilja gave a small smile. "Perhaps I am drawn to him because I sense his strong connection to the earth and his animals. It's difficult to explain my fascination. Sometimes it even puzzles me. I have known him a long time. We played together as children."

"Truly?" Peri sounded intrigued. She studied the beautiful land where the man walked. "His dwelling is made from the trees of the earth. It blends in with the forest."

As the man Grey worked about his snow-dusted dwelling Lilja saw the new groove beside his lean cheek, the vast sorrow in his eyes ... eyes that were far seeing and that used to crinkle with laughter. She shook her head. There were not many days he gave in to laughter any more.

She sensed he looked back to a time of his past. A happier time in his life, and then he turned from her and the wistful moment was gone.

"Lilja, did you hear me?" Peri asked, shaking her arm in gentle exasperation. "Come with me down to the faerie pool -- let's go sit in the sun and dip our toes in the cool waters. Dear one, you stand here with me but you are far away."

Lilja patted her friend's hand. "Peri, you always worry." Hesitantly, she admitted, "Sometimes when I go out there into the earth dimension," she lowered her voice, "I wonder what would happen if I never returned."

Peri sucked in a breath. "Forever?"

"Yes."

"No, Lilja. You would be lost to our world. What if they captured you and wouldn't let you return? You would turn mortal."

"I go for short visits to the animals that are in need of healing. Why would they wish to capture me?"

"They have their humans to heal the sick

animals," her friend said. "Please do not go. I would have to come and find you."

Lilja laughed softly. "Dear Peri, you would step into their world again for me?"

Peri shivered but said, "For you, I would."

"Perhaps you should come with me another time," Lilja said thoughtfully. "I am certain the humans would appreciate your wondrous gift of life drawing and it might take away some of your reservations about them. Humans love to see the future, and with the pictures you could paint them, they would be enthralled with your talent."

"Surely you don't think I would welcome their attention," Peri said, turning a shoulder.

"No worries. If you were in the human world, I would be very concerned. It is enough that you create glorious paintings in Aisywel to document our rich faerie lore." Though in truth the painting that hung in the great hall of the high elder Lukais gave her a bit of a shiver. The eyes just seemed so terribly dark and penetrating, quite unlike the faerie elder she knew so well. She shook her head. "Go along now, in time I will meet you at the faerie pool."

"I will go, but I do worry about your preoccupation and restlessness. Especially now when Aisywel feels so different. So unsettled."

"Silly faerie," Lilja said fondly. "I am the same as you've always known, but I know what you mean. I see worried faces everywhere. One cannot help but hear the talk. Go along now. I will meet up with you," Lilja said.

Peri's face wore a worried expression as she waved and disappeared in a faint twist of blue sparkle.

Lilja pondered how human lives were merely a speck in the enormous scheme of life. Ever curious, she turned her attention back to the man. She was acquainted with the human expressions for joy, fear, frustration and pain, but at times it felt beyond her scope to actually grasp the effect of those emotions on the humans.

Lilja walked through the forest, hearing the sprites hidden beneath the leaves and grass as they encouraged all life in Aisywel to grow and continue on as usual, despite a palpable tension in the air. Lilja wasn't sure what had caused the sudden change in her dear, sweet faerie world, but she was certain the elders would sort everything out. After all, it had been that way for all time as she knew it. There were no ripples in Aisywel; life remained predictable and calm.

With Grey's face in her memory, Lilja sat on a small chair formed out of various twigs and branches outside her little cottage. She closed her eyes and began to sing. The healing song was an ancient ballad she knew from the time she was young. Raised with other children in the wee faerie nursery by the caretakers of the realm, she'd listened avidly to the stories told there, stories of times long past.

The world around them continually shifted, was shifting even as she sat here now, and there was a collective awareness that the time for all worlds to merge was drawing nearer. For some in the faerie realm, it presented a frightening prospect, and the elders were trying to keep everyone calm, but Lilja had always leaned more toward curiosity as she sensed changes in the world of the fae. At times she had a sense she could see things beyond all dimensions, but those moments were fleeting. She felt in her heart a time would come where there would be no division between the human world and the fae. For Lilja, it presented a curious possibility. But then, she'd never feared the humans and had been familiar with them from a very young age.

When she visited the animal creatures on the human plane, they became invigorated and grew well again. Singing was her most treasured skill in the fae world. When she gave her voice to song, the day did not dare to hide the sun.

Curious to look in on the sick horse at Grey's barn, she waved her hand gently through the air to create a portal. Even though she had woven her healing song around the once-spritely mare, her soul now barely flickered. It caused a deep ache in Lilja's chest. Sometimes this happened, and then that soul was lost to the life it knew.

Looking through the portal at Grey's solemn face, she sang to him as he gazed up into the snowy winter sky. Gradually, Lilja backed away from the portal and it faded into faerie dust. Her dear friend Peri awaited her down by the faerie pool. There would be time for more healing later. After all, Aisywel was a timeless place and the worlds around her were easily accessed.

∞ Chapter Two ∞

The woman's husky voice carried on the wind. Grey Maddox had heard that haunting song for the last three nights. The words were indistinguishable, carrying an almost Celtic sound as they wound around him. And, just as he had the last three nights, he walked across his yard and tried to follow that voice to its origin. There wasn't a house for five miles. He owned fifty acres, so that meant someone was camped on his property or playing games with him. Who that might be he didn't have a clue. And who would be out in this building snow-storm anyway -- a hiker who had gotten lost in the hills? It just didn't make sense.

He'd swear the voice came from the horse barn, but when he slid open the door and walked inside, the song gradually faded. He proceeded down the darkened aisle to check his animals. A faint flicker of blue light caught his eye and it seemed to be coming from Everstorm's stall. Drew quickened his steps.

The mare had been ailing for three days, and the vet hadn't been able to discover the source of her illness. They'd done everything they could to make her well, and now to make her comfortable, but he had just about resigned himself to losing her. It was always tough losing an animal, his guts twisted into knots at the thought, but Everstorm ... she was special.

As the snow swirled and temperatures plummeted, so did his faith in the mare's recovery. It wasn't unusual to have a blizzard in April, but he'd wished it hadn't happened now.

Grey opened the stall door. He had camera monitors hooked up and had been watching her from the house while he grabbed something to eat; nothing had changed since then. She still lay listlessly on the straw bedding, eyes half closed. He knew if they couldn't find out what was wrong, he would have to decide whether or not to euthanize her. He was a horseman and he had dealt with death before, but he couldn't bear the thought of her suffering.

Grey knelt by the mare, ran his hand gently over her neck, and rubbed her jaw the way she used to enjoy, but it barely stirred her interest. He sat with her in the clean straw he'd built like a nest for her, but except for the slight rise and fall of her sides, she remained motionless, barely clinging to life.

Finally, Grey stood, fists clenched, then strode back outside. He felt helpless in the face of this mysterious illness. So much for modern medicine. Blood work, lab tests ... nothing had turned up. How could that be?

He looked up at the sky, now a dull gray void.

"Will you take everything from me?" he demanded.

An answer came on the wind in the faint strains of a song.

***

Grey went back inside his ranch house, a medium-sized, comfortable cabin that he and his brother Drew had built only last spring. He stomped the snow from his boots, untied them and left them on the boot warmer by the door.

He moved about efficiently, making himself a cup of strong coffee and putting together a grilled cheese sandwich. He knew it would be another long night. The time between midnight and four in the morning was the longest for him. It was difficult staying awake in that strange half-light just before dawn.

As he passed by the large screen monitor for Everstorm's stall, something caught his eye. He leaned down and looked at the screen. "What the heck!"

Drew shoved his plate back on the counter, grabbed his rifle from the wall, shoved on his boots and shot out the back door. Running to the barn, Grey pushed the wood sliding door open just enough to squeeze inside and moved quietly down the aisle. Carefully, he used the toe of his boot to gently slide the mare's stall door open.

"What do you think you're doing?" he demanded, but there was no one there except the mare. Feeling a little foolish, but knowing he'd seen the shadow of someone moving about the stall, Grey looked quickly around. He stepped back outside the stall, gave a quick look up and down the shadowy barn aisle then walked back down the aisle. He checked each of the horses, touching them as he passed them, looking inside their stalls.

He had seen a woman in the stall with his horse! Dark-haired, she'd lain fully across his sick horse from the mare's belly to her neck. That was odd, to say the least, and dangerous.

He ran his flashlight around and in every stall, the bales of hay stacked in the far end of the barn and the tack room. Nothing.

He had been a sheriff's deputy for over eight years; he dealt in facts and hard reality. He didn't just "see" things or imagine things that weren't there.

Grey rubbed the back of his neck.

Again, that sad, haunting song.

He was either incredibly tired or he was going crazy.

He stood stock still, the air inside the barn almost pulsing at him, as if charged with a strange energy. It swirled around him like wispy tentacles. Out of the corner of his eye he saw a darting shadow, but when he turned, there was nothing but a thin string of light, which vanished seconds later.

Shaking his head, he looked back inside the mare's stall. Everstorm moved her legs, and then her head and neck. Dumbfounded, Grey watched as the mare stood and shook herself as if she'd merely risen from a nap. She whickered softly then came to him in the doorway. Gently, she nuzzled his jacket with her upper lip.

Putting his rifle high up on two hooks outside the stall, he walked slowly into her stall so as not to startle her. "Everstorm, girl, how are you feeling?" He checked her eyes and noted that their color was good. Then he gently pressed his thumb against her gums and let go, holding his breath as the color quickly returned to normal. Lastly, he gently pinched a fold of her skin at the neck. He'd been worried earlier about dehydration. The skin went back immediately when he let go. Amazed, he went over in his mind what she had looked like earlier. He was confused but nonetheless grateful. He would need to make a call to the vet so he could come and check her out.

Had he just seen a miracle?

Grey made sure the mare's water bucket was full with an electrolytes mixture, then closed the stall and hurried back toward the house to call the vet. Rounding the corner of the barn, he sighed. The cabin lights were out and everything looked dark, which meant he'd lost electricity. He made his way around to the back of the cabin and into the small shed that housed his generator. He'd test run it only that morning, just in case the storm kept going, and now it started on the first pull of the cord. He activated the main switch and attached the heavy cord to the plug inside the shed.

Once more inside the cabin, he knelt down by the panel box and one by one flipped the switches to the "on" position. The lights came back on, the refrigerator hummed and the woodstove fan whirred once more.

Grey lifted the house phone but there was no dial

tone. He looked at his cell phone, but he didn't have any bars on that either. He needed to simply hunker down for the escalating storm. Hopefully, his mare would still be improving in the morning. He didn't want to think about the alternative.

How had she disappeared? He frowned as he replayed the scene in his mind. A trick like that was something Annie might have done, hiding out in the barn until he came looking for her. He smiled but then chided himself. What a foolish thought -- Annie was gone, dead three years in a freak accident.

Grey left the coffee and sandwich on the side table, no longer hungry.

∞ Chapter Three ∞

"Lilja."

She turned quickly from the portal.

"You've been playing in the human world again." Lukais, the faerie high elder stood behind her, gently disapproving, his long white beard swaying against his chest. As long as Lilja could recall, Lukais had looked out for her and advised her. He was the most esteemed of the elders who maintained faerie rule with the help of the powerful Aisywel crystals. She always valued his knowledge and guidance, but now a tiny spark of rebellion burgeoned inside at the disapproval she sensed in him.

He had guided her through many lessons, taught her about faerie law, and had been instrumental in her moving into her own dear little cottage. Many faeries chose to live communally, but Lilja had always been uncertain if that choice was right for her. Once her own little cottage had grown up in a small field to accommodate her every need and wish, she had been very happy and knew it had been the right choice. She loved her vibrant flowers, ferns and trees. It always surprised her how very perfect the cottage was for her, since she didn't have much talent for building structures.

Now she smiled at the elder and said, "I merely sing to comfort the animals. Surely there is no harm? It brings me such joy and the animals respond so well."

"Of course they respond, how can those dense creatures not respond when a light-as-air-faerie sends them healing energy? However, it is not appropriate for you to use your healing skills in their world. They have their own means of seeing to their sick."

Her smile faded. "Then why am I gifted in this way?" she asked passionately. "Surely I have not been given these skills so that they may go unused? Long ago, it was discovered my soul gift was for healing. Am I restricted to Aisywel, where none get sick?"

"Lilja, we have talked of this many times. There has been an ages' long agreement between the faerie realm and the human one; no interference and no intermingling."

"By whose rule?" she asked. "When I think of our rich faerie history, there has been much intermingling and even intermarrying between the two species."

His head went back and his blue eyes grew cold. "It was decreed by the eldest of faerie elders," he said. "Long before you were born into this realm.

Long before I was born."

"But others have stepped into the human world. Pandimora --"

He looked shocked. "It is forbidden to speak of Pandimora," he said sternly. "Was she ever heard from again? We fear the worst for our dear Pandimora. Would you wish to be lost to the faerie realm also as she was? If you were to fall off into the deepest dimension of forgotten you too would be soon gone and not remembered."

Lilja did not respond because she was really uncertain of the answer. In truth, she could not recall the exact details of Pandimora's departure. Pandimora was a vague memory, an old faerie story she'd heard long ago. Lilja regularly immersed herself in the rich history of the realm of her birth, but she felt deeply troubled she could not remember any stories about Pandimora.

It chilled her to think of being locked out of the faerie realm, the world that claimed her as their own, and yet another part of her rebelled at her gift going to waste.

"Lilja," Lukais said more gently, "you do our world much good with your healing. The fireflies thrive and show their happiness through their brilliant beauty. The rabbits and small animals express their appreciation each new day. Surely your home here is enough for you? How could you even look for more outside our enchanted borders?"

"But the animals here do not need healing. The humans and their animals have a real need." Turning once more to look at the snowy scene in the human world, she frowned. "They truly need me," she added softly, caressing the gilded edge of the portal.

"And what do you think your existence would be like in the human world?" he asked reasonably. "They have extremes of hot and cold on your body, emotions which would confuse you, and their world is in turmoil, certainly a dangerous place for someone as gentle as yourself."

She looked at him curiously over her shoulder. "You sound well acquainted with their world."

He stood with his hands behind his back. "As a boy I played a dangerous game. I too became fascinated by the humans." His mouth became firm and straight. "But I overcame that weakness and realized my true place was here in Aisywel."

"You lived in their world?" That fascinated her. "Did you fall in love?" she asked, wide eyed.

His blue eyes flickered and a faint spark of light shown in the pupils before it faded. "When I was very young, I ventured out to their world and stayed for a time. I almost fell under their spell, but in the end I found their world a confusing bombardment of noise and wisely returned to Aisywel. I had a hard time readjusting upon my return. My faerie memories had begun to be replaced with human world memories."

"Perhaps that is what happened with Pandimora and she chose to stay," she suggested softly.

"You have friends and loved ones who are truly happy you live in this world. They embrace you with their energy and their caring. I fear Pandimora may have fallen under the spell of the decadent human world. Don't you see? It does not matter about

Pandimora!"

She looked at him, shocked. "But surely there is no proof? Surely we in Aisywel would know of such a misfortune to another faerie." She clapped her hands, her eyes wide with excitement. "Perhaps she found a human to love and did not want to return."

"Never!" The elder waved his hand and suddenly looked quite irritated. "Why would she seek a human when there are brilliant faeries from whom to choose?"

Lilja stepped back in surprise at his vehemence and suddenly recalled the portrait of Lukais that Peri had painted. The painted eyes looked as dark and stern as Lukais' gaze did now. Peri had a knack for capturing the true essence of a soul.

Lukais voice softened and his face once more became serene. "Why would anyone choose to leave the faerie realm? Sunshine and rainbows, no wars or fighting. Life here is always pleasant and we never die the human death."

Lilja frowned, feeling ungrateful in the face of the vibrant beauty around her. She looked at the portal. Due to her healing skills, she had always been very sensitive to changes in the energy vibrations around her. She wondered -- did he feel the stirrings of unrest? She had always shared everything pertinent to Aisywel with Lukais, but now she felt a reluctance holding her back.

"In their world you would not be protected by magic as you know it here," Lukais said. "You would grow old, and most importantly, our world may forget you as many seem to have forgotten Pandimora."

Lilja frowned. It would be expected to miss a dear friend, and surely Pandimora had had many friends, but no one ever spoke of her. She caught her breath. It was almost as if she did not exist. For some reason her name had popped into her thoughts earlier, but she could not recall her association with her or any memories of Pandimora that she could draw upon. That created a vague uneasiness within her. She pressed her lips together tightly. Was she being affected by her own preoccupation with the human world? Is this what happened when she spent so much time thinking about that other world and spending time there? Would her memories of Aisywel be erased?

"What do you remember of Pandimora?" Lukais asked now, stroking his chin.

Lilja stared at the vast sky above them, saw the perfect blue and pink butterflies flitting in the constant, perfect warmth of the day.

"I cannot bring any memories to my mind," she said. She looked up earnestly. "I am sure I will remember. Perhaps if I study harder, I will come across stories of Pandimora."

Lukais smiled and merely patted her hand. "Lilja, sometimes memories are meant to slip away from us. This is one of those times."

She shook her head. "It is very strange. I remember every day on Aisywel, but I cannot bring up any memories of Pandimora. And yet I know her name."

"And that is how the faeries here would remember you, Lilja, if you were to leave."

"They'd forget me?" she asked, aghast.

He nodded. "Another reason to stay well away from other worlds."

"It's just that the human world appears so lovely and different." She stepped against the portal behind her and her bare foot slipped through. Lukais quickly gripped her wrist and pulled her back.

"Do be careful," he chided.

Lilja bit her lip, discomforted. She was sure she'd seen a flash of anger in his eyes. But had she? Faeries did not get angry at their own kind.

She pondered their conversation long after the elder left the university room.

Almost unable to help herself, she felt drawn back to the portal. She watched as Grey piled firewood in his arms and disappeared into his dwelling. She wondered about the solitary life he now lived; she had seen his earlier life and knew he had not always been like this. Lilja couldn't seem to help her preoccupation with this man. It did almost feel as if she'd been bewitched!

She leaned closer, turning her attention back to the horse. Reaching her hand through the portal, she soothed the horse, her fingertips barely stroking the horse's silky hide. The mare's liquid brown eyes watched her, as if grateful for her healing skills.

"There, there." She crooned a special, even more powerful healing song. The words flowed from her throat in rich, velvety notes. Reaching with her other hand, she placed both palms on the mare's neck. Through the vibration of her song, life energy pulsed to the mare.

And then Lilja fell through the portal.

***

Grey pushed against the wind and blinding snow, putting a gloved hand out so he could feel the barn door handle. He pushed it open then, using his flashlight, he moved to Everstorm's stall at the end of the aisle.

The mare lay once more in the fresh bedding, but her head was up and her eyes were alert ... and a woman lay with her cheek against his mare, her arms around Everstorm's neck.

Dressed in a light summer gown, she lay pressed against the mare's belly, her feet dangerously near the horse's hooves. Short, glossy dark hair with a wing of shocking pink splayed across her cheek and neck, concealing her face, but he was sure it was the same woman as before.

Grey bit back a curse, afraid that if the mare tried to get up she'd step on the woman and crush her bare feet. Carefully, he spoke to the mare, then knelt beside her and reached forward, gently grabbing the woman under her armpits and pulling her toward him. Just as he pulled the woman clear, Everstorm came to her feet. Grey let go of the woman when he noticed faint blue sparks of light where his hands touched her.

She suddenly drew in a deep, ragged breath and pulled away from him to kneel in the straw. He blinked, the blue light that had moved between them beginning to fade. He looked into her face, mesmerized for a moment by the glow around her.

"I didn't mean to startle you," she said, her voice bearing a faint Irish lilt.

Grey mentally shook his head. "What the heck --? What are you doing in my barn?" he demanded.

"You could have been seriously hurt."

Apparently unconcerned with his anger, she flashed him a brilliant smile. "The mare is well?" She stood and moved toward his horse, her movements as fluid as if she danced on air. Bemused, he stared at her bare feet.

Danced on air ... Grey groaned. What was the matter with him?

She was not very big, but she stood next to his big draft mare without fear. Everstorm proceeded to arch her neck and seemed to bow her head down to the woman, who pressed her palm to the mare and gently rubbed her forehead.

Startled by the mare's uncharacteristically mild behavior, Grey said, "Here now, get away with your bare feet, you'll be trampled."

She turned to him with wide eyes, and he stared fixedly at her. She literally glowed. Eyes, smile, her skin...her greenish eyes. There was something familiar about her ... something tickled a memory for him, but he just couldn't grasp it.

He gave up trying to define what he was seeing. He reached forward, took her elbow and led her from the stall. He quickly released her elbow when blue strings of light curled around his hand.

"What the heck is going on? You can't just come in here and think to mess with my horse --" he broke off as she shivered. "Geez." He unzipped his heavy canvas jacket and pulled it off, putting it around her slim shoulders. He looked at her bare feet. "One of us is nuts here. Am I imagining this? You're dressed for summer or a Renaissance fair, I'm not sure which, and there's nothing on your feet. How the heck did you even get in here? It's freezing outside!"

"Oh, yes, the snow! I would dearly love to see the snow," she said, apparently delighted by the idea. Her accent wove around him like a musical note. Clutching the jacket about her slim shoulders, zipper undone and open sides flapping, she hurried away down the aisle toward the partially open stable door. Before he realized her intent, she'd stepped outside and disappeared.

Hardly able to believe she'd just run out into a snow-storm, Grey ran after her. He needed to regain control of the situation. He was an officer of the law -- maybe she needed a doctor? He cursed. The phones were out.

He reached the door seconds later and stepped out into a winter white-out. Snow swirled in vicious snow devils whipped up by the wind, dropping the temperature even more. He couldn't see anything and any tracks disappeared as soon as they were made.

"Hey!" he called. "Hey, ma'am!" He ducked his head against the combined sting of snow and sleet, pulling his shirt collar up as the skin on the back of his neck got pelted. The wind seemed to stop suddenly for a moment, and he saw her sitting in the snow, knees under her, face uplifted to the sky as she leaned back on her hands. He quickly reached her and pulled her to her feet. She proceeded to dance from side to side in the snow. Grey lifted her in his arms.

"It's beautiful!" she exclaimed, reaching a hand toward the heavens.

Lurching toward where he knew the cabin to be,

he finally spotted the welcome glow of his living room lights. Grey climbed the two short steps to the covered porch and, stomping his boots, turned sideways next to the door.

Away from the blinding snow, he noticed that same crazy blue light, but now it formed a hazy glow all around them. He turned his head to both sides, and it seemed as if they were in a spotlight. What the heck! "Open the door," he yelled, trying to be heard above the wind.

She reached down and fumbled for the doorknob, and then they were inside. He pushed the door closed with his foot and brought her over to a chair by the fire. Luckily, he had a nice fire burning in his woodstove and a good supply of seasoned firewood at hand. They wouldn't freeze. He deposited her in the chair and then knelt in front of her, sitting back on his heels to stare at her. The soles of her feet were bright pink. He yanked his gloves off, picked up one of her feet and then began to rub it, surprised to find it quite warm. He let it go.

"What is going on?" he asked. "Did you see that crazy light?"

Despite her face being pinched and white with cold and snow melting into her hair, her eyes were wide with excitement. He scooted back a little further. Being this close she literally took his breath away. Grey stood, needing some space.

When he looked back to her eyes, now bluish green, he found them still bright with excitement ... or fever. Her eyes were unlike any he'd ever seen.

He was in good shape but he found himself breathing hard. Adrenalin? Staring at her heart-shaped face with its pointed chin, he was for once at a loss for words. She looked like someone out of a storybook, a pixie with her dark brown hair and that swathe of pink hair over her eye.

"The snow is even more glorious than I imagined."

Grey shook his head with disbelief, trying to regain his sense of equilibrium. "You could have died out there," he snapped. "With that wind bringing the air temperatures down to minus zero temperatures, people die in squalls like that." He looked at her dress in disbelief as she pushed his jacket off her shoulders. "And dressed like that, you stood even less of a chance."

She reached down and began to rub her feet. "But we're in here with a nice warm fire." She put her hands out in front of her. "It's as warm as home."

Grey narrowed his eyes and frowned at her. "So let's hear it," he said, "what were you doing out there?"

She avoided his glance.

He gritted his teeth. "Tell me how you happened to be on private property, in my horse's stall, in the middle of this freakish snow-storm?"

"I was worried about the mare," she said then added happily, "and now she is healing."

He looked askance at her. "And what would you know about it?"

"I knew she was sick, so I came to see that she recovered. I will soon be on my way," she added matter of factly. She pushed the damp hair away from her eyes. "I will trouble you only for a few moments more."

Grey frowned. "You're not going anywhere until I find out exactly what's going on." He looked at her suspiciously. "How did you even know my mare was sick? I don't exactly live in a highly populated area in town."

"It's a gift I have."

"You know when horses are sick?" he asked skeptically.

"All animals." She shivered delicately. "And plants."

Grey stood and moved over to the couch. He gathered up a bright blue and red quilt and brought it over to her. She pulled her feet up onto the chair and he wrapped the quilt around her and tucked it under her feet. His nostrils twitched. She smelled like lavender and ... and sugar cookies, for heaven's sakes!

From her cocoon, she grinned at him. He'd never seen eyes exactly that color, almost a merging of clear, luminescent blue and green, eyes that observed him with a deep piercing regard. She looked to be somewhere in her late twenties, a little younger than he was.

"Your hair is dripping," he said abruptly. He went and retrieved a towel from the bathroom. When he returned, she was still smiling.

"I am sorry to trouble you," she said again, apologetically.

He held out the towel. "Why are you so cheerful?" he demanded irritably. "Don't you get it, you are in trouble -- and besides that, you could have died."

She seemed to consider his words seriously and

then shrugged her shoulders. "But I did not die and no harm has been done."

"It's like you're from another planet," he muttered. "You have no idea what could have occurred."

And she did appear totally unconcerned. Grey looked away from those mesmerizing and attractive eyes as something stirred in him he hadn't felt in years. He shut down that thought and turned to tend to the fire.

∞ Chapter Four ∞

Lilja was still trying to get used to the different earth vibrations. At first when she'd made contact with the horse, her body had felt so weighted and sluggish that she'd had the urge to sleep. Now, as she grew more attuned to the atmosphere and the different air vibrations, she took a deep, filling breath into her lungs. She almost laughed aloud as her chest expanded with the breath. But she pushed back the gurgle of laughter. Grey would not appreciate it, that much she could see from the frown on his face. He remained quite serious and perhaps angry at her. That sobered her quickly. She did not wish for him to be angry.

She held out her hand. "I am Lilja," she offered. "I am truly sorry to have disturbed your quiet day."

She watched the frown deepen on his face. Although quite a handsome face, even by faerie standards, she already knew from observing him the frown was a habitual expression for him. He accepted her hand, turned it over, then reached for her other hand and did the same, as if looking for something. Puzzled, she let him turn her hand palm up. He let go.

"Today has been anything but quiet," he said. "You've got to realize this is highly unusual, you appearing in the middle of a snowstorm virtually miles from anything?"

She nodded in agreement, but that seemed to only deepen his frown.

"Are you in trouble?" he asked gruffly. "Hiding out?"

The dark glossy cap of her hair bounced as she vigorously shook her head. "No. Certainly not."

"What's your last name?" he asked.

"Just Lilja." She leaned forward just a bit, staring up at him from her warm cocoon. He was tall, towering over her quite easily. She closed her eyes a moment and listened to his aura at the heart chakra.

Loneliness, bent on survival, hard as stone, but a little something still there that might soften.

She settled back into her cocoon, satisfied. He had a good heart. A good heart was always an important factor when dealing with any life force. Even a faerie needed a good heart.

He moved away and picked up an iron rod to poke at the flaming logs in the firebox, causing tiny red sparks to snap in all directions. Fascinated, she put her hands out to try and catch the sparks. They looked like little fireflies, similar to the ones found in Aisywel.

He grabbed her wrist and gently pushed her

hand back into the quilt. Putting the rod aside, he stepped on a stray spark as it dropped to the wooden floor.

Briskly, he said, "Let's begin again -- how did you arrive here?"

"I dropped down in."

He put his head back and looked up at the rafters. "Dropped down in from where?"

Lilja chewed her lip. "I arrived here by accident." It had been accidental, her falling into this world. "I was in Aisywel and I meant only to comfort the horse, but I fell through into your dimension." She frowned. "I'm not sure why that happened. Perhaps something changed because of the storm?"

"Dimension?" He looked at her in surprise and then caution. "Where is Aisywel?"

Lilja knew humans believed in the faerie realm less and less as time went on, and by the look on his face, she suspected he did not believe in faeries at all.

She waved her hand. "My home, but surely it does not matter. I must now be off and back to where I belong." Almost reluctantly, she pushed the warm quilt from her shoulders and stood. She shook out the skirt of her gown so the material covered her toes. Her feet felt quite warm and toasty now on the wood floor.

He looked out the window at the snow hitting the glass. "You can't go anywhere," he said patiently. "We're in a total whiteout, the main roads are unplowed and the phone lines are out ... I'm afraid you're stuck here until things let up."

"I must go back to where the horse is in the

barn," she told him simply. "Then I will leave."

He put his hands on his hips. "You can't go right now."

This was not going as Lilja had expected. "But I must. It's the only way I can get back to Aisywel and leave you to your day."

He tilted his head. "Explain to me how you plan to get back to -- to Aisywel."

"I will climb back through the portal."

"Portal?"

"A portal is a --"

He put his hand up. "I believe I know the basic idea of what a portal is, I'm just not understanding -- you're saying there's a portal in my barn to this Aisywel?"

"I know, it can be confusing," she said sympathetically. "Not your barn specifically -- this land opens to several portals."

Under his unwavering stare, she added, "I will show you." She walked toward the door but was suddenly stopped by his hand on her arm. Feeling the tickling of energy move from his hand to her arm and then around down to her fingers, she stared at the energy connection of little blue sparks, and looked up at him in surprise.

"That is highly unusual," she said.

Narrowing his eyes, he released her. "Yeah. Do you want to tell me about it?"

"It is an exchange of energy."

"We exchanged energy?" he asked, one brow lifted.

She admired his straight jaw line and sighed. He was really quite handsome. She nodded earnestly.

"Yes, all living creatures are made up of energy. It doesn't usually manifest in such a way, but then this is the first time --" she bit her lip. It was the first time she'd ever touched a human.

"First time?"

She shrugged. "First time I've noticed such an energy exchange." If he asked her a direct question she could not lie, but she wondered what he would do if she told him she was a faerie? Would he feel he must detain her? What if he wanted to keep her here? No, he would not harm her.

"I am sorry, but I must leave now." She had already stayed far longer than she had planned.

"You can't go outside," he said firmly. He ran a hand through his dark hair, and several strands fell over his forehead. He appeared to be somewhere around her own age, but she knew humans did not age the same way as faeries.

"I must return to the horse so I can show you the portal," she said reasonably.

"Not dressed like that." He moved back to the fire and grabbed his jacket then picked up the gloves he'd dropped on the floor earlier to rub her feet. "I'll go check on the mare and you stay here until I get back." He pulled aside a lace curtain on the door and stared out into the night. "It's pretty dark out there now and the snow is really piling up. I won't be long."

"I'll come with you," she insisted, moving to stand behind him.

"You want to climb back through the portal," he muttered then sighed. He walked over to a door in the wall and opened a closet. "Here, put these on if you insist on coming with me. I'm not going to be responsible for you getting hypothermia."

When he turned around, he held out a long black coat with a hood that had fur around the edges. Lilja accepted the long coat, running her fingers tentatively over the fur.

"Do you have an aversion to animal fur?" he asked. "It's fake."

She smiled at him. "I will wear this."

"Then come on, time's wasting." He ducked back into the closet.

Lilja nodded enthusiastically. "I'm very pleased with her progress," she said, putting her arms in the coat.

"Here," he said, holding out boots. "These boots should fit. And a pair of socks." He shook his head. "How the heck could you be out here dressed like you are? It's like you dropped out of the sky."

"Portal," she said absent-mindedly, pulling the socks over her feet and then placing her feet in the boots. She had observed humans enough to know how garments went on the feet.

"Gloves." He handed her heavy wool gloves for her hands and she fumbled with them. He took the first glove. "Hold your hand straight out." Carefully, he pushed the gloves on, making sure her fingers were lined up properly. "Next one." She held out her other hand and he put the glove on that hand also.

"Thank you." She beamed at him.

He looked at her gravely. "Button up." He indicated the top buttons of her coat.

She looked up into his face and wondered why he frowned every time she smiled.

"Do you know you glow?" he asked.

"I do?" That intrigued her. "Like a firefly?"

He stepped away and cleared his throat. "Yeah, something like that. Stay close to me," he warned. "I don't want you getting separated in this storm. The barn isn't that far but you can get disoriented in the snow."

She nodded.

He opened the door and they stepped outside into the blowing, swirling snow.

***

Grey wasn't too sure about her coming with him to the barn. He'd have rather she stayed inside, but he wasn't sure he trusted her to stay put in there, either. Strangest thing he'd ever come up against. How could she have seemed almost impervious to the blistering cold with her bare feet and flimsy clothes? He assessed the increasing strength of the storm around him. Luckily, he had provisions to last him for quite a while and being on vacation was an added plus. He did hope the storm passed quicker than the four days they predicted, though, because he was wondering if she needed some kind of medical intervention. Was she delusional? Her story was as full of holes as Swiss cheese and her behavior just didn't add up. She acted like snow was a novelty and the cold no big deal. And then there was the portal thing.

Portals. He sighed.

"Come on!" He raised his voice above the wind as she drifted away from him. He grabbed her arm. "Stay close to me."

Once inside the barn he stomped his feet, turned

to her as she followed, and he slid the door closed behind her. He watched in amazement as she quickly shed the gloves and coat and then the boots and socks. Lightly, she ran to Everstorm's stall.

"Wait."

Grey got there moments later, not even surprised to see Everstorm cozying up to the woman. Lilja. Unusual name. Warily, he watched her pat the mare and talk in a low, crooning voice.

"Everstorm's always been more taken with men," he observed, again checking the horse for signs of illness or dehydration. "I've never seen her take to women."

Lilja smiled. "She knows I came for her."

He raised a brow. "So you say."

"And she is well now."

"And what do you know about her being sick before?" he asked.

"It was what she ate," she said simply.

Grey looked at her sharply. Trained in observation, he saw nothing suspicious in her clear eyes but of course he wanted to know what she meant. "How would you know? If that were the case, my other horses would be sick," he added.

Her bluish green eyes met his. "Perhaps they are."

He felt a deep, hard knot in the pit of his stomach. Something about the way she said that so solemnly made him walk out of the stall. He pulled his small, high beam flashlight from his jacket pocket. One by one he checked the stalls. There were ten other horses.

He finished checking one side of the aisle and

moved to the opposite side. As he did so, Grey began to hear that haunting song again. He stopped, turned, but she wasn't behind him. He opened the stall door in front of him and she stood inside the stall, her arms around his big colt Dancer, who seemed content to stand there with her.

"Lilja," he said. "How --?" he looked back at Everstorm's stall, then at her in with his colt. A weird tickle went up the back of his neck.

She turned her face toward the colt's deep black hide and began to sing the haunting song he'd been hearing for three days.

"It was you," he muttered. He didn't understand the words but now he understood how he'd thought the song sounded vaguely Celtic. It was partly her accent. He stood there for countless moments, then moved closer to his horse to check his eyes. Gently pinching the neck hide between finger and thumb, he determined the colt was slightly dehydrated. He hurried out to the tack room to prepare the same electrolyte solution for Dancer as he'd prepared for Everstorm.

"I know I sound like a broken record here, but do you mind telling me what is going on?" he asked when he returned to the stall and emptied the mixture into Dancer's water bucket.

Abruptly, she stopped singing.

"It's you I've been hearing the last three nights," he said.

She looked at him in surprise. "You heard my song?"

"I've never had anyone sing to my horses before. Of course I heard you singing."

She smiled at him now. "I whisper the healing, you hear it as a song."

"Have you been here before?" he suddenly asked.

She frowned, then nodded. "There was another time, one summer when your horse tumbled down a ravine --"

"You're kind of freaking me out now," he muttered. "So if you sang to my horse back then, how come I never heard you -- or saw you?"

"Perhaps at that time your ears were closed to the music. It is on a different vibration than what the -- what you might be used to."

"And now you're saying my ears are open?" he asked, clearly skeptical. "And my sight?"

She nodded solemnly. "Your ears, your mind and possibly your heart."

Grey turned away abruptly. "My heart -- yeah, right. Listen, I'm going to check his feed, make sure there's no mold, no bad hay -- in fact I'm going to withhold any grain until I have all of it checked."

"It's no longer here."

"What?"

"What made them ill," she stated simply. "It was ingested four days ago, a small brick that three of the horses had access to."

He looked at her sharply. "A mineral block -- three horses? So you're saying another one of my horses --"

She pointed to the last stall down the aisle.

Grey hurried down to the last stall. Princess Raven's stall. Heart in his throat, he opened the stall door and found her lying in the straw. Dropping to his knees, he ran his hands down her neck. Her eyes were closed. He checked the pulse in her neck and found it thready and weak.

"She was fine a few hours ago," he muttered.

Lilja knelt beside him and Grey watched as that faint blue light appeared between her hands and his horse's brown coat.

Not understanding and almost against his will, Grey said, "Can you help her?"

She turned to him, her smile gone, a sadness in her eyes as she bowed her head. "She is very special to you."

He nodded. "She was my wife's favorite horse."

"I will do my best. My gift seems --"

"What?" he asked, his voice almost hushed.

"Weaker."

"You're a horse healer," he said with sudden understanding. "A whisperer."

She looked almost startled. "Healing the soul is who I have always been," she said simply, "but the vibration is different in this -- here," she added. She reached out a hand to him and slowly he reached forward and took her proffered hand. Again, he felt that strange frisson, like an electric tingle that jumped from her warm hand to his. She frowned, pressed his hand on the mare's neck, then placed both her palms on the sleek muscle. She put her head back and closed her eyes.

And she began to sing, softly, her voice filling him, stirring in him a deep welling of tightly coiled emotion.

Grey stood up stiffly, watching her, hands in his back pockets and jaw clenched. He didn't understand his strong reaction to her singing. His nerves felt raw, as if every hurtful emotion of the last three years had been laid open.

The words of her song up to now had been hidden from him, but suddenly he understood what she sang in her strange, lilting voice. Emotions swirled around him almost like colors, and he wasn't sure he wanted to hear any more. He felt as if his guts were being wrenched out. His chest hurt as if he wanted to cry, something he hadn't done since the night Annie and their unborn son died.

I am a soul not unknown
and yet a soul who rides the wind.
I played as a child in the fertile soil of your backyard and mine
but now the storm has washed me to this distant shore,
and heroes there are no more
Oh, dragons and foxes and the rings of faeries-a-dancing they will come, they will come,
and the day will brew where your eyes alight on my true face, and all will be healed and
no longer will you fear the long silence of the night.

∞ Chapter Five ∞

Grey stood at the end of the barn. He'd checked the rest of the horses, and even Dancer seemed to be back to acting normally. Of course, she had sung to Dancer and the horse had perked right up. Grey had a hard time explaining to himself what he was thinking and feeling. Who was this woman with this -- this gift? How had she suddenly appeared as if conjured ... or was it true she'd walked through a portal? And why his place? Why now?

He'd heard of horse whisperers and healers, but she was different than anything he had ever seen. That soft blue light still radiated from the stall where she lay with Raven. He had not gone back down there since she began singing. His head was denying what was happening, and yet part of him yearned to go back down there and see for himself how she healed his horses.

Grey strode back down the aisle and stopped

outside the stall. That light glowed around her and his horse. She wasn't singing now, a respite for which he was grateful because her singing had stirred him up. He'd thought he'd conquered his emotions years ago but he felt like he'd been kicked in the gut. Why had the day of Annie's death suddenly come to the forefront of his mind so all that pain and loss were no longer hidden?

He kept coming back to the question, *who was this woman?* Something just felt unreal to him. God knew he was a man with his feet firmly planted, but he almost felt disoriented by her being here, as if he was no longer sure of things he'd taken for granted his entire life. Who talked about portals and used an unearthly blue light to heal sick animals?

She'd said she would go back to Aisywel. Where and what the heck was Aisywel?

Was she conning him? That could be, but how then had his horses suddenly gotten better? He could see it with his own eyes. Even Raven looked less distressed. Grey had gathered all the mineral bricks from the horse's stalls and dumped them in the corner of the tack room. He wasn't taking any chances. He would get all of them tested just in case, but if she was right, the one that had made the horses sick was already gone.

The only other possibility could be she had planted some kind of toxic substance in his barn, but what could possibly be her motive? His investigative training kicked in, going around and around with possibilities and motives, but he had no ready answers.

***

Lilja stared at Grey as he stood outside the stall. His face was shadowed, his doubts showing on his face. She could do nothing to allay his suspicions. She sighed. She should not have stayed so long in the earth realm. There would probably be repercussions. She chewed her lip. What could they do to her, chastise her? Make her promise to stay away from the earth dimension? No. That would be a punishment she couldn't bear. Lilja turned her loving attentions to the horse, knowing it wouldn't help to worry over something that was now out of her control.

Tenderly, she caressed the horse's neck, ran her hand lightly over her forehead. She could feel the life force struggling inside the animal. There was more troubling this soul, she felt, than the toxic substance that had been ingested. There was a troubling weakening of the soul's desire to live. She could see the dark swirl of sickness around the horse's eyes and in her heart.

She sang very softly, encouraging the horse to rejoice in its life, her song requesting permission to aid her in getting well. Thus far, the horse had rejected the healing, and Lilja knew if this continued, there would be nothing more she could do.

Abruptly, she came to her feet. She swayed a moment, caught off guard by a light-headed feeling. She leaned her shoulder against the wooden wall, waiting for the weakness to subside.

An arm came around her shoulders and pulled her into a hard male body. Her nostrils flared, taking in Grey's scent, redolent of sweet hay and horses.

"Are you all right?" he asked, his voice deep with

concern. The concern touched something deep inside and she sank into it, closing her eyes to allow his essence to flow through her. Deep and vibrant, it helped restore her from the momentary weakness.

Feeling stronger, she nodded. "Thank you. The weakness has passed." She stepped away and pointed at the horse. "She needs you," she said. "I don't know why, but she's sick at heart. Only you can help her."

His face seemed to pale in the shadowy light. She felt the pain emanating from his life force.

"What are you talking about?" he asked.

"I don't know," she said in frustration. "She asks your forgiveness. It wells deep inside her, festering from the inside out. She needs something from you."

She saw him swallow. He stared at the ill horse with eyes darkened by pain.

"She was my wife's horse," he finally said. "I -- I blamed her for Annie -- my wife's death, and our unborn son. I was angry."

Sadly, Lilja nodded. "She feels that blame all the way to her soul. You may not even be aware of such thoughts, but she understands each time you look at her those thoughts lurk deep within."

"I'd never want to make her ill," he said gruffly, clearly appalled.

"Just as you give your other animals love, she too needs this attention. She wants your forgiveness."

Abruptly, Grey turned and left the stall, shoulders wide, back straight as he walked away down to the other end of the barn.

Lilja moved to kneel beside the horse, crooning softly, drawing her healing energy from deep inside, laying it over the horse like the warmest blanket of spring flowers, a colorful, lively blend of life and sun to make her well.

She left the horse to rest, knowing she had done all she could for now. As she left the stall, she moved down the aisle to look in on the horse Dancer. He seemed to be doing well, and that made her pleased.

"So what are you? A witch? An alien?"

Lilja turned to Grey, seeing the murky shadow of pain still clinging to him.

She sighed gently. "I am of the faerie realm. I heal animals," she said simply. "I go where they need me."

He made a snorting sound. "A faerie?" Disbelief.

Amused, she said, "You would believe I was a witch or an alien, but not a faerie?"

He looked taken aback, then a glint of humor appeared in his eyes. "Well, it's a big universe, so aliens wouldn't be too farfetched. Men and women practice witchcraft, but faeries -- like little people who live in the woods, fly around with gossamer wings -- not really my area of expertise."

Lilja burst out laughing. Twisting around, she patted her shoulders. "See? No wings."

"I see," he said. "No wings." He lifted a brow. "So you get around using portals."

She moved into Everstorm's stall. The mare stood in her stall eating a flake of hay, and she wickered a soft welcoming hello. Lilja moved to her side, touching her neck and shoulder, then walked toward the wall and through the portal.

Almost all the way through, she turned and looked over her shoulder at Grey. He called her name as the portal closed and dissolved behind her. She'd never forget the shock on his face.

***

The elder high faerie council was not pleased with Lilja, but for once she felt unconcerned for having disobeyed Lukais.

"It was the right thing to do," she said, her voice respectful but firm as she stared at the council of three elders. "I have healing skills and I must continue to use them."

"We are not disputing your right to use your skills, Lilja, and I think you know that," said Lukais, seated to the right of the other two council elders, Bernate and Matlei. "However, you know it is ill advised to intermingle with the humans and spend so much time in their world."

"There was no other way," she said. "The animals were close to death."

"That is the way of the earth dimension," said Bernate, his brown eyes compassionate. "Birth and death. Surely you know this."

"Of course, but I can make a difference, so I chose to act in a manner I felt was right."

"We will confer on this," said Lukais, and she knew the matter was closed for now.

Lilja was the last one to leave the university hall. She stood in the middle of the vast hall, the light shining upon her through the glass walls and ceiling.

It was strange to her that the elders were so concerned about her entering the human plane. It was well documented that for thousands of years faeries had intermingled with humans. Sometimes the faeries aided the humans and other times it was the humans lending their skills.

But now, they wished to keep the two races apart? Lilja had not yet been able to identify the shift that was occurring, but she felt as if something was being hidden. She wished she could pinpoint the discomfort that nagged at her. Even this meeting had felt rushed, as if it was hastily decided something must be done about her visits but that there were other matters that needed attention.

Lilja walked from the hall, wandering the forest as night fell like a blanket over the realm. She wandered through the trees, staring upwards at the magical wonder of faerie dust in the air, scarlet fireflies buzzing by her head and at her feet. The calm night enveloped her, the darkness healing the ache that twisted around her heart.

Lilja thought of Grey on the other side. She wondered how he was feeling and if he was still worried about Princess Raven. Lilja had given him the key to the mare's recovery. Even her healing skills could only go so far.

She might have returned to Aisywel undetected earlier, except that when she stepped back into her world, it was in the midst of the midsummer festival. She had been gone longer than she expected, having forgotten that transitioning between the faerie realm and human time created a vibrational shift that the faerie realm at times experienced as an atmospheric ripple.

The elder council had immediately been aware of her return and had requested her presence. It had surprised her when Lukais suggested she be reprimanded, and the other two elders had finally agreed.

And now her transgression would not be easily forgotten. She supposed that everyone in Aisywel must have been reminded anew of Pandimora's disappearance. But was that really true? She didn't remember anyone other than herself bringing Pandimora up in conversation. How could a faerie be so easily forgotten? Lilja had to wonder just where she had disappeared to in the human world ... or had she disappeared into another dimension? She seemed to recall that long ago faeries had speculated that Pandimora's soul gift had been stripped and that she'd vanished in a sprinkling of dust. Now Pandimora seemed to have been forgotten completely.

Lilja looked out now over the fire-lit lake and surrounding area where the festivities were still underway. Dancing, storytelling, games, puppet shows for the wee faeries. When had she begun to feel disenchanted or apart from this life? The restlessness had been growing for many years: fifty or more, she reasoned.

Perhaps Lukais sensed it, although he had never asked her outright. What could he do? Send her away so as not to create unrest among other faeries? Even her studies no longer consumed her as they once had.

And why was she different? Was it because it was rare for her gift to be called into use in her own world? Was that truly the root of her growing dissatisfaction?

In truth, she knew some of it had to do with *him*. *Grey.*

She had played with him in his time as a child, reverting back to her own childlike nature. There was something about him that pulled to her, spoke to her in a language that transcended both their worlds. As children, they had played games in the woods and hills, enjoying each other's company. No one had reprimanded her for coming each day to the human world, for she had slipped back into the faerie realm at dusk each night. And those had been good times, until the boy grew into a man and forgot about his faerie friends.

Lilja smiled in soft remembrance, and she slipped away from watching the faerie celebrations. She remembered instead her last sight of Grey, hand extended as he called her name.

***

Grey grappled with his disbelief over the woman Lilja melting into the wooden boards before his eyes. Her astonishing disappearance explained the strangeness of her sudden appearance on his ranch. How did flesh and bone dissolve into nothing? But then, she'd said she was a faerie, he reminded himself. *From Aisywel.*

Grey filed those bits of information to the back of his mind. He was a man with his feet firmly planted in reality; he believed in proof, evidence, things he could touch. How could he even begin to believe what she said was real?

Dancer and Everstorm seemed to have recovered from whatever bothered them, for which he was grateful. Had Lilja really made them well?

And what about Princess Raven? It made his heart ache as he stared at her in the stall, her eyes closed as she labored for breath. With a sigh, he thought of what Lilja had said. How could she know of his feelings about the mare? He'd been so angry at the time of Annie's death, blaming the mare, when in reality Annie's death had been no more the horse's fault then his own. Annie had been a grown woman, and she'd made the wrong choice in taking the horse out that day three years ago.

He walked into the stall and went down on one knee besides Raven. He stroked her neck, struggling to find the right words.

"I never meant to hurt you," he said gruffly. "Perhaps I have done some kind of damage in holding all this anger inside. Anger about Annie taking chances, losing her and then the baby. Being the mare you are, I know you did your best to bring her safely back, but it wasn't to be. I'm sorry you've suffered because of how I reacted." He almost felt foolish talking to the mare like this, but something deep inside made him continue. "I want you to get well, Raven. Forgive my short-sighted, bullheaded ways."

He sank to the straw then sat with his back against the wall, turning off his flashlight and shoving his hands in his pockets, hunkering down as the wind howled outside. In the shadowy stall, he kept company with the horse, hoping that maybe Lilja was right and that maybe she would return.

That thought made him come up short. But then he relaxed. *He did want her to return.*

***

Lukais, her champion and mentor for all of her life, stood before Lilja in the great glass domed hall.

Except for a deep sadness in his eyes, his face remained impassive. She knew a decision had been reached by the high elder council. She braced herself, her friend Peri by her side.

"There have been several in the faerie realm who played with danger throughout our long history, courting the friendship of the humans, seeing no harm in merging the worlds, mixing our immortal blood with their lesser blood. This must come to a stop or the faerie realm itself will be endangered." He looked down at Lilja from his position above her on a raised platform. "There will be no more visits to the outside world. No more intermingling with humans. You will find another way to use your gifts for healing."

Lilja came to her feet, shaking off the cautioning hand Peri put on her arm. "That is unjust. What is it you fear?" she exclaimed passionately. "I have never been put in harm's way through the actions of any humans."

"Then you have been fortunate," Lukais said. "We cannot take the chance that others will be tainted by your curiosity and perhaps follow your lead. The council has made its decision: the portals will be sealed. There will be no more interactions."

Lilja felt as if she were breaking deeply apart inside, a horrible rending in her heart. "You cannot make me choose -- such a choice should never be asked."

"Lilja!" Peri cried, but Lilja ran from the great hall, feeling as if her chest were on fire. *The horses*, she thought, *the horses!*

"It cannot be. It cannot be!" She ran through

portal after portal, leaving behind sharp, snapping flashes of light, and then she reached her sweet little dwelling. The door opened for her, and she ducked her head under the crimson ivy she had draped over the doorway only that morning. She closed the intricately carved door with its polished brass fittings, acknowledged the greeting of the deep blue morning glories as they smiled at her from the windowsill.

Wildly, she looked around her bright and sunny room, her books lying beside the window seat where she curled up to read faerie stories, her bed with its soft fern bedding ... what was she to do? Dare she leave all this behind, the only life she had known? Perhaps she could defy the elders and find an escape before all the portals were sealed. She sank into the corner window seat, her lovely moss pillows cushioning her body with their springy softness. A tear escaped down her cheek. She rocked herself back and forth, thinking, planning. How could her gift for healing be bad? What was wrong that she would now be a prisoner in the lovely Aisywel when she wanted to explore the worlds outside?

Calming herself, trying to think clearly, she closed her eyes. She kept seeing Grey's face as it was when they were children, and then the worry in him when his horses were ill. She had thought she had all the time in the world to get to know Grey, but they were taking that away from her. Her loyalties felt torn.

"The portals. They will close the portals," she muttered.

Peri burst through the door, out of breath and wild-eyed with fear. "Lilja!" she cried. "Lilja, please do not do it." She came to a halt beside her, white-blonde hair flying about her shoulders, her blue eyes damp with tears.

"Peri, dear Peri, calm yourself," Lilja soothed, continuing to rock back and forth. She leaned her forehead against the glass window, staring outside at the deepening twilight.

"I can't. I know what you are planning. The portals are being sealed now. I am afraid for you," she said. "I don't want to lose you as Pandimora was lost. Gobbled up by the human world."

Lilja turned in the seat and stared hard at her friend. "Peri -- think -- how do we know that Pandimora is lost? What do we even know about Pandimora? I can't recall anything and yet I feel as if I knew her! Perhaps she is living quite happily among the humans. Maybe they sealed the portals that she used and she can't come back. Did anyone ever look for her and try to bring her home?" Lilja looked up into her friend's face. "Maybe," she said darkly, "maybe she knows something we don't and she doesn't want to come back to Aisywel!"

"What?" Horrified, Peri stared at her. "That cannot be. Aisywel is all perfection and wonder. The weather is a constant perfect temperature, the sun shines just the right amount, and every one of the fae knows how fortunate we are to live in this enchanted world where all our needs are met."

"Not all our needs," Lilja muttered, thinking now of the unrest in her heart. She ducked her head down, resting her chin on the fern pillow. "Maybe there is a darker side to Aisywel. Haven't you felt the odd vibrations of late? My heart is aware of uncertain undercurrents stirring, but I can't fully grasp what it is I feel. Just a wisp of a feeling. I am increasingly uneasy."

Peri lowered her voice and moved closer. "Lilja, certainly you do not think the elders would do anything dastardly?" but her voice wavered a bit.

"I know, it is difficult to even entertain such a thought," Lilja agreed, but her mind kept working. "But what if every perfect thing in Aisywel is all a lie? How did Pandimora disappear and no one even remembers her? If she were well, surely she would come back and tell us?" She looked at her friend, saw the fear in her face. "Peri, tell me something. What memories do you have of Pandimora?"

"Well, that she was a faerie and -- and --" she stumbled to a halt, looking confused.

"You have no memories, do you? In fact, until I mentioned her name to you previously, you did not remember that she existed in our world?"

Peri frowned. "Well, that might be true, but surely she did exist here. How else would her name seem familiar to me?"

"I don't know. It all seems very strange to me. How can a memory come to a blank wall? Deep concern gnaws at me over this. There must be a reason she didn't come back."

"Maybe she is ... " but Peri did not finish.

Lilja paced her cottage, walked over to a ruby red mirror with a blue glazed surface. Using both hands she turned the mirror on its back, staring at the glass. Long ago it had been a gift from . . .

someone, -- but who? Frustrated, she couldn't remember. But it was created for her so that she might watch the animals of Aisywel. Little did the elders know she had kept it hidden for many years, having discovered another use for the seemingly innocuous surface. Now, she passed her hand over its rough surface until gradually a snow scene took shape.

"Lilja," whispered Peri, but Lilja turned and put a finger to her lips. "Watch," she said.

She looked through the swirl of snow at the cabin deep in the pines. Looking inside, she saw Grey, but she could not see the horses. That puzzled her. Had they taken a turn for the worse since she had left? She could not see inside the barn.

"They have closed the portal in the barn," she muttered, pressing her fingers against her chin. She moved back to the portal in the snowy fields, but that suddenly went blank also. She pressed her hands against the surface, trying to create blue sparks of energy to reopen her private window into the earth realm, but it remained firmly closed.

"They have closed the portals," Peri said. "You cannot leave, they have locked the way."

"I can't see the horses," Lilja said, trying to still a sense of panic. "What if they are gravely ill once more? I should have stayed," she fretted. "I should not have left until I knew they were all well."

"Be thankful, Lilja, you might have been locked out of your own world instead of the earth dimension. You are worrying about human things," Peri added slowly. "Even now when your life is in turmoil and the elders have chastised you, you worry about them."

Lilja tried again to bring an image to the blue surface, but it remained frustratingly blank. "I need to return."

"To the earth realm?" Peri squeaked, eyes wide with fear. "What if you are trapped there?"

"I will find a way to return to earth even if I cannot come back here."

"I still do not understand your fascination and dedication to that place." Comprehension suddenly lit Peri's intense blue eyes. "It is him, isn't it? The one you call Grey?"

"I want to get to know him and I want to experience what it's like to live there. I had planned to do this slowly, but now -- I can't seem to let him go."

"I can't believe you kept this secret. You would abandon your life, your faerie family. You know there will be no going back if you pursue this course." Peri slipped an arm around her shoulders. She bit her lip. "There is a way," she admitted in a low voice. She turned away quickly and walked to the door as if she would leave. "No, never mind."

Lilja stared at her friend then ran across the room after her. "How?"

Peri took a deep breath, keeping her voice low. Hesitantly, she said, "It's very dangerous, even for a faerie."

"Tell me."

"The lake."

Lilja blanched at that. She could not swim. In fact, most faeries she knew could not swim. Peri was an exception.

"There is a portal in the middle of the lake," Peri said in a whisper. "At the very bottom. I found it one day while I was swimming. I never told anyone. I believe it is ancient."

"You know I can't swim."

"But I can." Peri closed her eyes, pressing her fingertips to her forehead. "Maybe you can go each day to visit, to determine if you really do want to stay there, but you must be back by dusk, and no one will be the wiser."

"How?"

"I'll help you."

***

Grey stared outside. The snow had not let up for three days. Between the accumulation of four feet of snow and the continuous blowing and drifting, he knew there was no sense plowing his driveway until the storm blew itself out. When it all settled down, he'd get his track loader out and set about clearing the roads and pathways. Right now he was making do with a narrow path between the barn and the house he kept clear with his snow blower.

It wasn't the first time he'd been snowed in, but it was the first time he'd been alone. The last time, about seven years ago, he hadn't minded being snowed in with Annie. Back then all he'd had was a small two-room shack; they were lucky the roof hadn't caved in under the weight of the snow, but they hadn't cared. They'd snuggled under the covers for most of the two day storm and found a most interesting way to occupy themselves.

In the last three years, he couldn't think of anyone he'd want to get stranded with in a snowstorm. He felt like his life had come to a screeching halt that day three years ago, and he had concentrated on his job as deputy sheriff and on his horses ... until now.

He hadn't been able to get Lilja out of his head.

She was the first woman he'd really felt an interest in since Annie's death. He'd had lots of time to think in the last several days. He'd concluded that maybe he needed something else in his life. Maybe he needed someone to care about, perhaps even someone to love. He knew he was getting ahead of himself, but there was just something about her. He'd never met anyone so happy and uplifting. It was as if the sun followed her around. Never one to be whimsical, Grey grimaced and shook off his fanciful thoughts.

He rubbed the back of his neck, looking up at the ceiling then at his watch. Almost time to go and check on the horses. They were all doing well, except for Raven. She'd wavered back and forth for the last three days, though she'd seemed to perk up a bit after he'd spent time in her stall. He was at his wit's end as to how to help her. He'd done everything he could. He kept wishing that Lilja would return. Maybe she could make the difference in his mare getting well.

But she had not returned, and his barn no longer hummed with that pulsing energy nor had he heard any haunting melodies in a sweet lilting voice. Grey had to wonder where this Aisywel was. Didn't faeries live in the forest and hidden places underground? His knowledge about such things was extremely limited. Right now, with the storm, his internet was down, so there was pretty much no outside communication, except for his old ham radio.

Part of him wanted her to come back, but the other part, the lawman part, knew she could turn out to be big trouble if this was all some kind of elaborate scam. But then, why would anyone pretend to be a faerie?

He still had a difficult time wrapping his head around the idea.

Once the roads were passable, he'd go into town and stop in at work, check out the mug shots and the missing persons' database. But he knew that nothing he found there would explain her disappearing into a wall.

Usually he and his brother Drew talked out things they had trouble with, but this, well, he'd probably have to be literally out of his mind to mention this to Drew. How do you tell someone -- anyone -- that your horses were healed by a faerie from a magical place?

∞ Chapter Six ∞

Lilja had never experienced such terror in her life. Not even when the big black cat chased her through the human world in the deep jungles when she was just a wee faerie and she thought she would be eaten.

Peri pulled her down and down and down into the depths of the lake. Lilja trusted her very dear friend, but that did not lessen her fear. As Peri dove deeper through the dark green water, her hold on Lilja's wrist felt like a steel shackle.

Peri had warned her to hold her breath, and then they had slipped into the warm, swirling water. The lake always looked enchanted from the shore, glimmering with blue and aqua lights, fireflies skimming its surface at night, butterflies and shimmering dragonflies during the day.

Lilja kept her eyes open, hardly mindful of the brightly colored fish that swam past them. Down they moved past a lone mermaid sitting on a rock, until finally Peri put her face close to hers and pointed below them.

Trying to gather what remained of her wits, Lilja looked down at the portal in the lake floor, a round, bright blue depression against the dark, sandy lake bottom. It seemed to waver gently back and forth. Peri pulled her until they stood on the edge of the portal. When Lilja just stood there, Peri put her hands up, as if to say, *are you going or not?*

Lilja quickly hugged her dear friend and put her feet into the middle of the portal. She fell into it and out the other side.

***

Lilja looked all around but the white swirling snow made it difficult to see. She lifted her arm, and the once graceful drape of her gown was stiff and cold against her skin. Having come through the portal wet, her clothes were quickly freezing on her in the earth dimension.

She could just make out a dark shape ahead and hoped it was the barn or Grey's house. The wind subsided for the space of seconds, and she saw it was the latter. Forcing her legs to move, she tried to put her arms around herself, but that seemed to drive the cold deeper into her skin. She had never experienced such an icy cold in her life. Her teeth began to bang together and she could not control them at all. Very, very slowly, she tunneled through the snow toward the welcoming light shining through the glass windows. She clenched her jaw, but her teeth still clattered. Her head began to shake, and Lilja realized as she managed to climb the first step that her entire body was shaking uncontrollably. Hazily, she knew this was unusual since faeries were generally impervious to extremes in temperature.

Reaching out with both hands, she gripped the ice-slick handrail. Somehow, she managed to pull herself up the second step and onto the covered porch.

Three more feet.

The stiff, frozen material of her dress scraped against her legs. She tried to turn the door handle, but her hands were so numb they would not work properly. Lilja put her head against the wood door, felt the ice on her hair crinkle and break into little pieces that went down her neck. With both hands on the door handle, she leaned her weight against the wood and it opened. She fell inside and lay on the wood floor. Knowing she had to move, she managed to roll away from the door and pushed it closed with one bare foot. Using her elbows, she pulled herself over to the heat of the burning fire. The fire was roaring and it felt so good, but then she began to feel even colder as the ice melted and she lay shivering in her wet, thawing dress.

Remembering Grey's words about the weather, Lilja knew she needed to get out of the wet garment. Feeling very weak, she sat upright and struggled to untie the sash at her waist. The wet and partially frozen knot refused to come undone. Looking around, Lilja saw a knife on a small table beside the chair. She opened it then carefully cut the sash material. When she tried to close the knife, her cold fingers turned clumsy and she caught the blade against the skin of her small finger. She watched in horrified fascination as bright red began to stain her dress and then drip onto the wooden floor.

Grabbing the sash, she wound it carefully around her sliced finger. Its throbbing made her feel sick to her stomach. She did not bleed in the faerie realm. Almost overwhelmed by the new experiences, Lilja just stood for a long moment, afraid she would fall down. When the sick feeling subsided somewhat, she gripped the arm of the chair to steady herself. Awkwardly, she pulled her heavy, sodden dress over her head and dropped it to the floor, trying to rub away the crimson stains on the wood.

Kicking the sodden dress toward the mat next to the door, she sat down on the small soft rug in front of the chair, pulling the quilt Grey had wrapped her in before over herself as she curled up. She put her arms around her body, letting the heat finally warm her chilled flesh. Exhausted, she remembered the reason she had come ... the sick horse.

And Grey.

She just needed to get warm. She dropped her head against the chair and very softly, she began to sing.

***

Grey turned his head, straining to hear over the whistle of the wind through the barn timbers. Had he heard something?

He walked down the aisle toward Raven's stall and pushed the door open. "Lilja?" He shone his flashlight into the stall, but she wasn't in there. Surprised by his strong sense of disappointment, he proceeded into the stall to check on the mare. At least now she was standing and showing some interest in drinking. That was always a good sign. He ran a hand down her neck, feeling the muscle under her skin, then shining the light briefly into her now bright eyes. Hope began to rise in him that she, too, would recover. It also made his heart beat faster. Had Lilja returned? But where was she?

Grey pulled the stall door closed and now there was no mistaking Lilja's husky voice in the air around him. He began to feel a barely perceptible pulsing of energy in the barn, though not as strong as it had been three days ago. Anticipation wound through him.

Grey's smile grew, but then he cautioned himself; Lilja was still an unknown, and he needed to tread carefully until he got more information about her. He checked all the stalls, made sure the horses were set for the night, and then closed the door behind him. He admitted to himself his own eagerness to see her again. Had she returned? She was not in the barn.

Lilja's song was faint as it carried the wind, weaving a spell with its haunting quality. It drew him, put hope and at the same time fear in his heart. Who was this magical woman? Was she really what she represented herself to be?

Grey frowned, looking all around him as he made his way back to the house. Any footsteps would be quickly wiped away by the wind and blowing snow. He stepped up on the cabin porch and was keenly disappointed when the song faded away. He opened the door and stepped inside, turning to close the door, stomping snow from his boots. Something caught the toe of his boot and he looked down to see a sodden ball of material on the floor. For an instant he froze. Lilja's gown, stained with scarlet.

Grey shoved the door closed and quickly zeroed in on Lilja fast asleep by the fire. Relief flooded him. She'd pulled the quilt half over her shoulders. Her head rested against the chair, her short dark hair in wet strands about her head, her back to him.

The glow of the fire played over her light golden skin.

Grey noted three tiny spirals inked in light blue on her right shoulder.

He strode forward. "Lilja."

She jerked, as if he'd awakened her, but did not move otherwise. He knelt beside her, touched the skin of her shoulder. She was cold. Quickly, he went into his bedroom and opening drawers, found a top and bottom of insulated long johns. They'd be big, but it would work. Carrying them to the living room, he knelt beside her again.

"Lilja," he gently shook her shoulder. "We have to get you warm. Put your arms up, I want you to put these on."

He pushed aside the quilt, exposing her skin. Taking a deep breath, Grey eased the insulated top over her head. She raised her arms as he guided her hands into the sleeves, noticing his hands shook slightly. He pulled the top down over her and it settled around her hips.

"What have you done to yourself?" he asked, gently examining the wrapped finger with what looked like the fabric from her dress. It was soaked with blood. "Let's get these clothes on first. Can you stand?" He helped her stand, and she suddenly looked up at him, her bluish green eyes wide and startled. "It's okay," he said. "You need to put these clothes on and get warm." He caught a glimpse of slim legs and stifled a groan.

"Grey," she said softly and smiled. Her beautiful eyes lit up, and that smile went all the way to his heart. Then she frowned and looked down at the insulated long johns he held.

"Put them on," he said patiently. "Sit down in the chair and it'll be easier. I'm going in the kitchen to make you some hot tea and then I want to look at your finger."

"Tea would be lovely. Thank you, Grey." He turned, but she gripped his arm.

"Raven?" she said, alarm in her voice. "I am not myself. I came back for Raven."

"Raven is doing well now that you're here," he said.

She relaxed. "Good."

"I'll be right back."

Grey left her sitting on the chair, the long john bottoms in her hand as she stared at the wood stove. He frowned, wondering if faeries could get sick. Then he stopped. Had he swallowed the faerie story hook, line and sinker? Did he really believe faeries existed?

Grey rubbed his forehead. He conceded the strong possibility she was something other than human. Now there was an admission he'd never imagined himself making; that there might really be faeries.

Grey made a cup of coffee while he waited for

the tea water to boil. He put a spoonful of honey in her tea and a little milk then walked back to the living room with both mugs.

Lilja sat upright in the chair. She had put on the long johns and she looked much better than when he'd first found her moments ago. Her hair had dried into dark spikes, the pink in front sticking straight out, and now she sat cross-legged in the chair, watching him as he approached, her face expectant. He had to smile at the picture she made.

"You're smiling," she said, apparently approving.

"I'm smiling at you," he said. "You look like a pixie or something." He hesitated. "Is that the same as a faerie?"

She nodded. "That is also an appropriate term."

He leaned toward her, placing her mug of tea on the small table at her elbow. "Be careful, it's hot. Now let me see your finger."

"I am bleeding."

He thought she said it in such a strange way, as if perplexed.

Grey lifted a brow. "Don't faeries bleed in Aisywel?" Okay, he was buying the story then, at least for the moment. He was surprised how happy he was to see her again.

"I have never seen it happen," she said. "I used your knife to cut my sash and my finger got in the way." She shrugged and lifted her tea mug with her other hand. She closed her eyes. "This is surprisingly good. Almost as good as Mah Shiethe's."

"Glad to hear it," he muttered. "Who is Mah Shiethe?"

A fond smile curved Lilja's lips. "She was

mistress of the kitchen when I was a small child."

"Hmm, so I would guess she knows how to make a mean cup of tea?"

"Well, a delicious cup of tea," she asserted. "Mah Sheithe had a gentle heart."

"Lift your hand," he said.

"It is fine," she said dismissively. "I am sure it is already healing."

Grey frowned. "I still need to see it. It looks like it bled a lot. It must be deep. I keep that knife pretty sharp."

Lilja held out her hand and Grey pulled up a stool to sit in front of her. Carefully, he unwrapped her finger. She had wrapped it too tightly and the tip was faintly blue. He sucked in his breath when he saw the cut. It was a very deep slice between the joints. "You're lucky you didn't cut your finger off," he muttered.

She put her head close to his as she tried to look also. An intoxicating scent of lavender wound around his nostrils. Grey blinked and shook his head sharply.

Lilja let out a small squeal. "It's not healing!" Clearly shocked, she looked askance at him.

"Don't ask me, I don't know about faerie healing. Maybe you can sing to yourself," he suggested.

She lifted a brow, her clear blue green eyes mesmerizing when seen so close. He found himself sinking into them. For a second, he saw twin flames of light in the pupils. He blinked hard.

"Are you making a joke of this?" she asked, trying to suppress a smile.

"Well, if you sing to my horses and they get well,"

he said reasonably, "why not use some of that magic on yourself?"

"Magic does not work that way. It has to be a selfless act toward another."

"So you can't make yourself well if you're sick?"

She shook her head no then took another sip of tea. Grey went into the bathroom and grabbed some peroxide, gauze, tape, butterfly bandages and antibiotic ointment.

"And faeries don't get sick," she called after him.

He returned and sat back down in front of her.

"This needs to be wrapped properly. When this storm is over, you're going to need a tetanus shot. Have you had one recently?" He grimaced at his own question. "I don't suppose they have tetanus shots either in -- in Aisywel?" he said.

"Tetanus? I don't know what that is."

"And you never get sick?"

"No." She sneezed and looked at him with wide and surprised eyes. Then she started laughing.

He grinned. "Sweetheart, I certainly didn't do that. Are you warm enough?"

"Yes. Although when I first came, I was quite cold. I was very worried if I would make it safely inside your home."

Grey rested her hand on his thigh, palm facing up, wadded some paper towel under her hand and poured a little peroxide on the cut. He carefully dried it, smeared on antibiotic gel, followed by the butterfly bandage, wrapped it with gauze and carefully taped the gauze in place. "Be careful not to hit this," he cautioned. He stared at her slim fingers pulsing with that faint light just under the skin. They looked like any other fingers, except for the blue sparks when he touched her and when she'd healed his horses.

"How did you get so wet?" he asked. "The last time you were here you were perfectly dry."

"I needed to come back," she said. "I needed to see the horse. I couldn't leave her when she had been so ill." She looked away from him and bit her lip. It was the first time he'd seen a worried expression on her face.

"Lilja?"

"I am in trouble!" she blurted.

Grey's chest tightened, but he waited patiently to hear the rest. Did she have a rap sheet? Was she running from a toxic relationship -- an old boyfriend? His shoulders tensed. It had been a trick, after all, her seeming to dissolve into the wall.

"The portals have been sealed," she said. "The elders have forbidden the faeries to mix with your kind."

"My kind?"

"Humans."

She was still going with the faerie story then. "The elders found out you were coming here and they want to put a stop to it?"

She nodded, her eyes wide.

"Then how did you manage to get back here?"

"It was very -- you have a word here that doesn't exist in our realm." She scrunched up her face, tapping a finger against her forehead. Suddenly, she smiled. "It was tricky."

He clenched his jaw, his cop senses kicking in. "Share with me how tricky."

"My friend Peri, who is a very good swimmer, knew of an old, old portal deep in our enchanted lake. She had never told anyone else about it."

"Okay," he said slowly. "So I'm assuming Peri then told you about the portal in the lake?"

She nodded.

"You had to go into water to come through the portal?" he asked in disbelief, a cold wave coming over him at the thought.

"Yes, all the other portals were locked. I couldn't see Raven and I was worried she would die. I had to find a way to come back."

"So you wanted to come back for Raven?"

She stared at the flaming logs in the woodstove. "Of course."

"You swam to the bottom of the lake?"

She shook her head no. "Like most faeries, I can't swim."

"Then how did you get out?" Tensely, he gripped the extra gauze and tape.

"Peri is the exception and is a very good swimmer. She told me to hold my breath and she pulled me to the bottom of the lake."

If Grey had not been watching her closely, he would have missed the flicker of fear. "She pulled you down into the lake," he said incredulously, swallowing his own reaction. "It must have been terrifying for someone who doesn't swim."

"I was very scared," she confessed. "But it came out fine."

"Did you ever think that maybe a horse's life wasn't worth you going through such an ordeal?"

"No, I never thought that," she said indignantly.

She came to her feet and whirled around. Grey leaned back, feeling as if he'd been hit by a forceful wind. "I can see you don't understand," she said, crossing her arms in front of her. "My healing work is very important to me," she said distantly, turning a shoulder to him. "No one but Peri understands."

"Lilja," he said gently, "I am grateful you have helped heal my horses, but I would not want you to endanger your life to do so. That's the basis of my concern."

Her lip trembled.

"I would miss you -- your visits," he managed, swallowing the fear at the back of his own throat. "And my horses would miss your healing songs."

Lilja turned to him, her dark hair swinging across her cheek, her eyes large and bright. "I would miss them terribly also."

He let out his breath, again almost mesmerized by her bright, clear eyes. "I wouldn't want you to die trying to come back. You said you were in trouble. Tell me what trouble means in Aisywel."

"The elders held a meeting and forbid me to come here again," she whispered. "They are afraid I will be stuck here or lose my immortality. In our faerie history, somewhere in our time, another faerie disappeared into your world. It is not spoken of, but no one has ever seen her since. But I wanted to come," she said fiercely. "I have a gift to heal and I must use it." She tightened her lips then blurted, "And I knew I would miss you too, Grey, if I couldn't come."

Grey pushed back his own exhilaration at her words, cautioning himself to go slowly.

"Why can't you use your gift in Aisywel? Don't you have animals there?"

"The animals are all enchanted. They don't fall ill."

"You have a healing gift in a world where no one suffers illness?" he said slowly.

"Yes. I have been coming to your world since I was a small faerie," she said. "Why should I not continue to come? It is my choice."

"Maybe they're afraid you might want to stay here," he said.

"Yes." She sat back down, pulling the quilt about her shoulders again. She leaned her head forward and the pink wing of hair fell again into her eyes.

"I can see your gift means everything to you," Grey said. "How often do you come here to heal animals?"

"Over the course of many, many earth years."

"And you go other places?"

She nodded. "When they call out to me in their distress. Sometimes the animals hide in the wild hills, but I can find them easily."

Grey felt alarmed, imagining her in the hills where there were big cats and other predators. "You don't mean you heal the mountain lions and bears?"

Lilja nodded. "Of course. If an animal is sick, I will help however I can."

"Have you ever run into danger with a wild animal?" he asked, squatting down beside her chair.

Lilja nodded. "Only once. I don't understand why, but a big black cat chased me in the jungles." She shivered. "It was very confused in its thoughts and beyond my healing gift."

"Lilja! It might have had rabies."

She shrugged delicately. "I don't know. Perhaps, if rabies is an illness that affects clear thought. It was when I first began healing animals."

"How old were you?"

"In terms you can understand, I was about six human years."

"Six years old?" Stunned, Grey rubbed his forehead. "Sorry, I'm trying to wrap my mind around this. This is a pretty fantastic story."

She looked at him solemnly. "It is not a story. Faeries do not lie."

He looked at her dubiously. "Never?"

"It's not possible. Grey," she said urgently, "I do not have much time. I must visit with Raven before the night is over, and then I must go back."

"But you've barely gotten warmed up," he protested, not wanting her to leave yet. "And how will you go back if the portals are closed?"

"I dare not stay long. If the elders discover I have gone against their orders --" She shook her head. "Peri will be waiting for me on the other side."

"In the lake? I'm worried, Lilja. It sounds dangerous." In fact, it sounded life threatening.

"There is no other way," she said decisively.

Grey made himself say the words he knew he should say. "Maybe you shouldn't come anymore. Maybe the elders are right to keep you safe in your own world."

She stood up. "They are wrong, as you are wrong to say that. I am going to see my Raven and then I am going back." She neatly folded the quilt and walked toward the door.

Grey followed her, caught her arm before she could leave the house. "You can't go out without a coat, boots and gloves." She nodded, and he went to retrieve the items from the closet.

"These belonged to your wife?" she asked when he handed her the same long black coat and gloves and boots as before.

Grey frowned at her. "No. They belong to my sister, Pam. She stays here sometimes and keeps clothes here." He hesitated. "How do you know about Annie?"

"I watch this world, Grey. I saw your pain and loss."

"That sounds like spying," he said harshly. "Or stalking," he muttered.

The compassion in her eyes made him sorry he'd sounded so severe. "We only see that which you would allow. I dislike seeing the pain and suffering your world feels. I wish --"

"What?" he asked as she hesitated.

"I wish I could remove the pain associated with human emotion."

"That would kind of defeat the whole purpose behind emotions. Don't you have emotions and feelings in Aisywel?"

"We experience joy and every day is as expected, full of happiness, and we dance to celebrate our life."

"It sounds like it's some kind of ideal society."

"Many are very happy."

"But not you?" he asked shrewdly.

She shrugged. "I have always been slightly different. I ask questions others would never voice, and I experience moments of doubt when I have been gently accused of self-absorption. My world is beautiful, calm and peaceful, and yet I ask for more." She actually giggled a little. "I am the only one who continually pushes against the order of the faerie realm."

"So you don't like order. Here we call them rebels."

Lilja smiled and did a little in-place jig. "Maybe I am a rebel."

"A faerie rebel," he said, and Grey smiled at her. How could he not? She was so full of life and energy. He actually felt something cold inside himself begin to thaw.

When she had donned the outerwear he opened the door to the cabin and looked outside. "Sunshine," he said in amazement. "This is the first sun I've seen in a week."

He stepped back so Lilja could precede him out onto the deck. As she passed him, he noticed again the glow that surrounded her. He found himself watching her as she walked ahead of him. She fascinated him with her story of another place, a parallel dimension. It sounded too fantastic. How could someone just suddenly drop into his world and present him with a reality he had never even thought existed?

***

Lilja followed the path to the barn, pausing now and again to enjoy the beauty of the sun across the snow. The sun's rays picked up the energy of the snow all around them, making the ice crystals shine with brilliance. She put her hand up to shade her eyes. "It's very bright and glowing with energy," she said. "The ice on the trees is breathtaking. We don't have ice or snow in Aisywel." She listened for a moment and turned in wonder to stare at Grey. "Isn't that a beautiful sound?" she asked.

"What sound?"

"The ice on the tree limbs. It's quite musical as the wind moves the branches together. It's like the chatter of the sprites where I live."

He looked amused by her observation.

"I never thought of that as music," he said.

Lilja shook her head. "You are not listening," she said. "Humans many times miss hearing the world that calls to them every moment of every day." She pointed up toward the barn roof. "Even the snow hitting that roof makes its own music. All of nature has a purpose, Grey. I love to listen to the animals when I am at home."

"I enjoy nature," he admitted, "but now listening to you I'm seeing it in a different way."

Just then a huge icicle detached itself from the barn and dropped like a dagger to the ground, standing straight as it embedded itself in the deep snow. Lilja quickly moved to the fallen ice, which was even with the top of her head. She ran her gloved hand over its twisted, rippled surface but Grey quickly pulled her back.

"Watch it," he said, looking up at the roof. "If one of those hits you, it could hurt you badly."

"It reminds me of the Aisywel crystals," she murmured. She turned and looked up at him. "Do you think your crystals carry the same type of energy as our crystals?"

"I don't know what kind of energy you're talking

about, Lilja. These icicles are pretty common. The cold air reacts with the warmer material of the roof, which creates moisture. Then it drips off the roof and freezes the moisture to ice. There's nothing magical really about the process, though I admit when we were kids we thought they were great."

She smiled. "Maybe you should go back to thinking like a kid."

"Maybe. What kind of crystals do you have?"

"The high elder controls the Aisywel crystals," she responded. "They are extremely beautiful and powerful. Aisywel crystals help keep all the worlds in balance. They were formed beneath the earth's core in ancient times."

He lifted a brow. "How many worlds or dimensions are there?"

"Many, many, many," she said, throwing her arms wide. "Your dimension is a small speck in the great universe. We monitor all dimensions for stability."

They reached the barn and Lilja put out her hand to open the barn door, but Grey's hand was there first, holding the door closed. She was between the door and his chest. She looked up at him, so close she could see the fine, dark whiskers on his chin and the thrust of his jaw. His eyes were deep brown with little gold flecks. Lilja found she liked being this close to Grey.

"Tell me again just how much observing you do of our world?"

"Quite a lot. I like to see how your kind interacts. But I don't understand your ways when extremes of emotion are brought into play."

He smiled. "Even I don't always understand the emotional aspects of this human life."

"Yes, it is quite complex. I have studied for years, but I believe observing is not the same as being in the moment of emotions."

"Don't you have emotional relationships in Aisywel?"

"No. We have soul connecting. This is a union that goes beyond what you understand emotions to be."

"And no one else is interested in exploring the human world, except for you and a few other brave rebels in your history?"

"That is true."

"I'd say it's pretty courageous for you to come here to a place that's foreign to you," he said.

"I love learning about the humans and their habits."

"But why would you watch me?"

She looked down. "I have known you a long time. At times I watch you when you walk out there." She pointed toward the hills. "Or when you ride your horses across the land."

"How can you see all that?" he asked. "How many portals are there?"

"There are many. Just as there are many of my kind."

"And are there other faeries who watch humans?"

"From time to time."

"So it's your own fascination about human life that's brought you here?"

"Of course. And your horses' illness. I'm drawn

to the animals. Sometimes we communicate. The horses are very intelligent. They see the fae in our real light."

Grey reached behind her and pushed the sliding door open and Lilja was almost sorry to no longer be in such close contact with him.

Lilja saw a man strong and hard working, a man who wanted to believe her but still had his doubts. She understood that.

"Faeries have watched your world since ancient times," she said. "Humans used to believe in the faerie realm, but as time goes on there are fewer who believe. When they stop believing altogether, there will be no more faeries."

"Lilja, that's pretty extreme," he said. "It's like you're saying our lack of believing will extinguish your world."

"We will still live but will no longer be seen. Our vibrations will no longer match or mingle with yours. For you, our lives and history will cease to exist."

They walked into the shadowy interior of the barn and Grey left the door open behind them.

"What happens when someone has a foot in each world like you do?" he asked.

She lifted her head and met his gaze. "A choice will need to be made." She knew it would be a difficult time if she were forced to make that choice.

The horses gently spoke their greetings as she made her way to Raven's stall.

The mare looked at her over the wooden divider and whickered softly as she bobbed her head. Lilja opened the stall door, leaving her outer garments on a small hook outside the stall. She put her hands out gently to the mare and wondered what she smelled like to the horse. Wearing the long johns that belonged to Grey, she imagined she now carried his scent.

"How are you, dear one?" she crooned softly. "You look so much better today than when I saw you last. I am so grateful you have let yourself be healed."

"Could she stop her own healing?" Grey asked behind her.

Lilja half turned to him. "Yes, she could reject the healing if she so chose. It is because she loves you that she accepted the healing." She tilted her head, smiling at him. "You look as if you have reservations about that. The cycle of life continues, whether humans or faeries believe fully or not."

"So there may be faeries that have doubts about the benefits of healing earth animals?" he asked.

"Many can't be bothered to cross over into this realm. Generally we are a very happy lot, but there is a small group of dissenters who live in a forest on a lower vibration, though not too far from my glen. They are gloomy all the time. They speak only of ill tidings and misfortune."

"That sounds like trolls or gnomes," he said, his mouth quirking up.

Lilja looked at him with surprise. "Do you know the trolls?"

"No, I was just -- there really are trolls?" he asked in amazement. "I'm still having a hard time believing you're a faerie, but when you disappeared into that wall -- that kind of freaked me out."

Lilja laughed. "There are many, many worlds you may know nothing about. We faeries are but a wee small part of it." She patted Raven's soft nose. "I believe Raven is well." She looked up at Grey. "You no longer need my healing," she said, feeling sad and happy all at once. She had accomplished what she had set out to do.

"Does that mean you're not coming anymore?" he asked, frowning at the wall.

Lilja looked at him in surprise. "There is no need if the horses are well. I used to be able to send them healing from the other side of the portal, but with the portals closing, that will not work."

"How will you know if they're sick again?"

"I won't, unless I come through the lake portal."

Grey sighed and shoved his hands into his jeans pockets. "I was kind of looking forward to seeing you again. I'll miss getting to know you."

As Lilja looked at him, she felt a little ache in her heart. "I will miss you also, Grey. I won't be able to watch you walk the hills either, and that makes me sad." She stepped out of Raven's stall. "But now I must go. If I am late in returning, the elders will know I disobeyed."

"But you said they don't know about the lake portal."

"Peri didn't think so, but at dusk each night all faeries dance by the light of the fireflies. If I am not there, I will be missed."

"Can't you say you were sick?"

She laughed up at him, greatly amused. "But I told you, faeries do not get sick."

He handed her the outerwear she had discarded.

"I am leaving, it is not needed," she said.

"Wear them until we get to the portal," he said. "I don't want you getting cold and then get into that water."

"It is only a moment in time. The water in Aisywel is very warm," she said, but she put the clothes back on to please him.

"I have to tell you, Lilja, I'm really worried about this lake business. What if your friend isn't there to guide you?"

"She will be. Peri would never let me down. And besides, how hard can it be to float to the top?"

He let out a long breath. "It's scary even thinking about that with someone who can't swim. You could panic."

"I will be fine, Grey, but your worry over my welfare shows the deepness of your heart." She smiled as they stepped outside into the bright sunshine. "I am beginning to understand a little how these emotions of caring and concern work from being here in this world. You love your horses and don't want them to be ill, and I could feel that emotion in you. You have been sad for many years," she said softly, reaching up to gently touch his face. "I wish I could heal you as I do animals. I would heal your sorrow and your fractured soul."

Grey grabbed her arm. "Now I have a fractured soul?" he asked, his voice indicated disbelief.

Lilja nodded. "It can be healed, Grey. Never fear."

"How would I go about doing that?" he asked. "That is, if I believed such a thing."

"In time, you will fall in love again."

He released her arm.

"I am sorry, that is very personal to you," she said, biting her lip. "I have studied your social mores but in truth, my knowledge is in the infant stages." She moved quickly across the snowy ground and made new tracks through the snow, tunneling out into the horse meadow. Lilja looked at the landscape, took three more steps and stopped. She pointed to a faint blue pulsing circle on the snow. "This is the portal," she said.

Grey looked down at the snow. "I never saw that before."

"It is an entry point to my dimension."

"How can you tell?"

Lilja traced the portal with the toe of her boot and the ground wobbled.

"I can barely see the faint blue color on the snow," he said. "I wish --" he broke off and looked away across the field.

Lilja noted the snow had stopped and even the sky to the west was beginning to clear.

"What is it you wish, Grey?" she asked, taking his big hand in her own.

He gave a groan. "I wish you could stay. For the first time, I've actually looked forward to seeing someone -- a woman -- again. It's been a long time since I felt like that. I've been hoping for the last two days that you would come back."

Lilja smiled with joy. "Perhaps your heart is doing its own healing," she said with wonder. "That makes me very happy. The healing of your horses has opened your own heart."

He turned to her and lightly moved to grip her elbows in his hands. "It's you, Lilja, who's opened my eyes to new possibilities. I am grateful you've healed my horses, but it's you I will miss."

Lilja felt that ache again near her heart, this time much stronger. She looked down, uncertain about the pain she felt, the emotion she saw on his strong face. "And I will miss you, Grey -- and Raven, Dancer and Everstorm." She pressed her lips together. "I wish I could stay longer, but I can't."

She pulled off the coat and kicked off the boots. She stood on the snow in her bare feet, wearing only the quilted top and bottoms. She handed Grey the garments, then leaned toward him and, standing on tip-toe, impulsively kissed his chin. He dropped the coat and boots, put his arms around her, pulled her against his chest and kissed her mouth. Lilja melted right into him, for a moment lost in the beautiful colors swirling behind her eyes as their lips warmed each other and began to heat to an almost unbearable tension. She could see herself wanting to stay here, and of course that caused a conflict with her faerie upbringing. She was not the first faerie to be attracted to a human, but she knew that could be a difficult path for both of them.

She dropped down to her feet, staring in wonder at the blue aura that whirled gently around them.

She held her hand up, palm toward him, watching in wonder as he put his larger palm near hers. Blue tendrils of light snapped back and forth between their palms.

"Will you be back?" he asked, his voice intense. She looked up into his face.

"Yes, if I can get back through," she promised. She bit her lip. "I will try to come tomorrow. I must go now." Quickly, she discarded the quilted top and then the bottoms. As she dropped into the portal she saw the flash of longing in Grey's expression. It mirrored the longing in her heart.

∞ Chapter Seven ∞

With a flash of blue light, Lilja, all golden skin and dark hair, was gone. Grey staggered backwards as a force of air pushed against him. The portal seemed to wobble for a moment and then settled flat into the snow. He put a boot against the faintly bluish snow, and he felt it give as if it were gelatin.

What if he stepped into that portal? Would he go to where Lilja was or would he end up somewhere else? He shook his head, still mystified by the entire encounter. He retrieved the insulated top and bottom where they lay in the snow, then the coat and boots. Would she really come back or would she stay in her world and he in his? He clenched his fists on the clothes. Already the ache of loneliness snapped at him, taking him by surprise.

"Grey, what are you doing out here? Everything okay?"

Grey turned quickly to find his brother Drew

walking toward him. "Drew. I didn't hear you --"

"I've been trying to reach you," his brother said, dark brows drawn together. "I figured you lost electricity."

"Well, I'm glad to see you. I was worried about you when they towed your truck," Grey said. "Is everything okay?"

"Yeah, it's been a crazy week, but things are leveling out. This insane snow finally let up, but I just looked at the weather station and they said another northeaster is heading our way. Since the plows just cleared the main roads I thought I'd drive out."

"You came up my driveway?" Grey looked for his vehicle.

"Yeah, well, your driveway is another story. My truck's buried about a thousand yards down. You're going to have to pull me out."

"I planned to get the track loader out anyway," Grey said. "I was just waiting out the storm. I left you a radio message."

"Yeah, I know. And you sounded kind of off so I thought I'd come out."

Grey grinned. "So where have you been holed up the last week?"

"That's something we need to talk about. Trust me, it will take some explaining." Drew looked around, eyes narrowed. "But it'll have to wait for another time because I have to get back. By the way, have you seen my partner Sara at all? She left me a cryptic voice message and I haven't heard another word. I'm wondering if I should start looking for her."

Grey smiled. "Knowing Sara, she's trailing a bail jumper or something. That woman is tough as nails. I wouldn't be too worried about her."

"I know, but sometimes I do worry about her. She's not as tough as she makes out. What are you doing out here in the middle of the field with women's clothes?" Drew asked, eyebrows raised. "And long underwear -- I'm guessing you have company?"

Grey put his boot to the edge of the blue snow that was now barely perceptible against the snow. The ground still wobbled a little.

"I don't think you'd believe me."

"You have no idea how I can stretch my imagination these days," his brother drawled. "You can talk to me, but if it's a woman, you know Mom will be squeezing it out of you."

Grey walked toward the cabin, the clothes over his arm. "It's a crazy story," he said over his shoulder.

"Tell me your crazy story and I'll share mine." Drew's eyes widened slightly as he looked at him. "Someone's knocked you for a loop." His brother's gaze grew intent. "At least tell me her name."

"Lilja." Grey looked up at the hills and then the sky beyond.

"Lilja," Drew mused. "Unusual name. Did she take off because I showed up?"

"No. She had to get back to -- to her place."

"Without her clothes?" Drew asked, indicating the garments he carried.

"No, these are Pam's."

Drew paused on the bottom step to the deck.

"You know, the sun glare off the snow was pretty bright, but I swear I saw someone out there with you."

The inquiry in his brother's voice was as clear as day.

"You'll have to let it go for now, Drew. I'm not sure I'm ready to relate what happened out here during the storm. It's still pretty weird to me." He walked up the steps to the cabin. His mind was on Lilja. Had she made it out of the lake okay? What if her friend wasn't there and she drowned? He swallowed, his throat feeling dry. No! She couldn't have drowned. He'd just found her.

"Grey, I can see you're in a bad way over this woman. When you're ready --"

"I know," Grey said, pushing open the cabin door. "I know. Come inside -- at least I can offer you some coffee."

***

Drew didn't stay long. Grey got the idea his brother was anxious to be somewhere or with someone. After he'd hooked a chain on Drew's truck and pulled it down the unplowed drive to the road, Drew had made him promise they'd catch up with each other later in the week. At least it gave Grey time to figure out a way to tell his brother the truth, as crazy as it would sound. Grey spent the remainder of the day clearing his driveway out to the road. Then he ran his snow blower over the paths to the shed, barns and utility shed.

His electric power was restored later in the afternoon, and as he looked around the barn and field, everything seemed back to normal. Just another snowfall in the Catskill mountains.

Except for the petite faerie with dark hair and pink highlights.

There had been many storms through the years, but he knew he'd never forget this one. He somehow felt marked by Lilja's unexpected appearance in his life. He felt as if he'd been roused from a deep sleep, and now he felt like he was missing something since she'd left. If what she'd said was true, her mission had been pretty selfless. She had been so concerned about his horses that she'd risked censure and possible drowning in her own world to come here. He was tempted to call Drew back, but then how would he explain a faerie? What would he say? His brother was as down to earth as he was and would think he'd gone loco if he started spouting off about faeries and other worlds.

Grey marked the portal area with a steel pin that he drove into the semi-frozen ground with a sledge hammer. He wanted to make sure he knew where she'd be coming through, if she came back.

His vacation didn't end for another five days, but he decided to drive into town anyway and stop in at work. He needed to put his mind at rest and check the latest missing person's database. He'd also call in on the vet and update him on what was going on with the horses.

He called himself a fool, but he needed to rule out every other possibility before he believed what his own eyes had seen. If it all turned out to be an elaborate hoax, he'd been taken in pretty completely by the entire show, and that thought turned his mood sour.

***

"Grey, what are you doing here?" asked his boss, Jon Huntley, as the other man entered the patrol room.

Grey swiveled the desk chair around from the computer screen and nodded at Jon.

"Checking some databases."

Jon had just won re-election as sheriff in the small town of Gatesberg and spent most of his time at the office. Grey had been doubtful when the clean-shaven and earnest Huntley had first shown up to run for the position five years ago. But, despite his sometimes annoying habit of being a stickler for the most minute details, Jon was a good administrator and knew how to get things done for the town and for the small police force.

"Looking for anyone in particular?" Jon asked, one eyebrow quirked.

"There was a woman out at my place. I just wanted to check our recent missing person files. I don't know why but her face was familiar."

"Was she passing through?"

"Seemed to be."

"Well, I was just going through those files myself. The older files are in my office, or you can use the main computer for the more recent ones. If you need any help, let me know."

"Thanks. Anything else going on in town?" Grey asked. Had anyone else seen Lilja?

"While you were off, you missed all the excitement," Jon remarked.

Grey swiveled his chair around, his senses alert. "What's that?"

"Mike Buel lost his patrol car to a fire. He brought in a guy dressed in survivalist gear after there were complaints of him acting erratic, running through town with a sword of some type. Mike took him into custody but the patrol car suddenly went up in flames. Poor guy went up with the vehicle."

"Geez, Jon, that's horrific."

"I know. There's an ongoing investigation now. Mike's on leave. They're trying to identify the guy, but no luck so far."

"Weird. I just saw Drew, and you'd think he'd have mentioned it." Grey shrugged.

"Well, that's the extent of it, except for the storm. We should be back on track in a few days. I'm taking over Mike's patrol for now. Listen, I'll let you get back to your research."

Grey nodded and spent the next two hours sifting through the files, but in the end the databases didn't turn up anything other than a lesson in frustration. Grey rubbed the back of his neck and sat back in the swivel chair.

Of course he hadn't expected to find Lilja in that database, had he?

"Find anything?" Jon asked as Grey walked through the main office on his way out.

Grey swirled the last of the coffee in his cup. "No."

"Do you want to file a formal --"

"No," Grey said easily. "If she comes around again, I'll get more info. Thanks. I'm heading out." He left the office, his mind preoccupied with Lilja. If she was a faerie, he couldn't expose her, but if she was delusional and lost or needed help ... right at the moment, though, he was the one who felt a bit delusional.

Grey paused on the sidewalk, staring up the small avenue with its quaint old oak trees lining the street, vintage street lamps and historic houses. The police station was right in the middle of town, next to the town square with its park and small lake. His brother Drew's and Sara's investigative offices were a couple buildings beyond the police station.

He had grown up in this town, and things like faeries you just didn't hear about here ... or anywhere. He sighed. Maybe, just maybe, Lilja was exactly what she claimed to be.

***

Early the next morning Grey let the horses out into their paddocks for the first time that week. They were full of energy, having been cooped up due to the snow storm, and they immediately began to run and play. He leaned against the rail, thinking of Lilja, feeling almost on pins and needles with anticipation. Would she return as she'd promised? What if she didn't show? No, he pushed that thought back. She'd said she would try to get back and he believed her. He wanted to believe her. But he worried about her coming through the lake portal.

As he watched his horses, he thought of her soft mouth on his. Even though her move had been bold for such a seemingly gentle person, stepping up to him and kissing him, her lips has been tentative and then hot and persuasive. Grey smiled, pushed his hat back and looked up at the sky. He spread his arms wide. "Lilja!" His voice echoed off the hills and came back to him. "Lilja!" He was feeling better than he'd felt in a long time.

He worked around the house all afternoon, and as dusk began to fall, he walked out to where he'd marked the portal. Some of the snow had melted and now it was hard to tell where the circle had been. He pressed the toe of his boot against the area and immediately felt a slight give. Would she come back as promised or would she be lost to him before he ever really got to know her?

Grey looked all around, searching the tree line to the east, wondering if there were other portals out there. How many portals were there? He strode across the yard to the barn, entered Everstorm's stall and walked over to the wall where he'd first seen Lilja disappear. He pressed his palms against the wall, but it was solid. Frustrated, he wondered how the heck any of this was possible. When night fell and Lilja didn't come, Grey began to fear that he'd never see her again. Never hear her singing. He pressed his fists into the pocket of his jean, a sinking feeling in the pit of his stomach. Maybe it had all just been too good to be true. For the first time in a long time, he'd been interested in a woman, and she turned out to be a faerie from a world he knew nothing about and couldn't access. *Great.*

***

Lilja jerked upright from her sleep, then snuggled back down into her ferns. She smiled. Faeries dreamed in such vivid detail that at times it was difficult to distinguish dreaming from reality. Without thinking about it, Lilja pinched her arm. A red mark instantly appeared. She was now truly awake. She frowned as a memory tickled her.

Pinching her arm had been a trick she'd known a long time, but she couldn't recall how she'd learned it. She didn't know of any other faeries who would pinch themselves to make sure they were awake.

During the night Grey had crossed into her slumber. His essence had wound around her as if his strong arms had actually enclosed her. She smiled, relaxing into the soft and feathery ferns, the warm night air caressing her. She recalled Grey as she'd last seen him; the surprise in his eyes when she'd kissed him. And the feeling that curled around her heart as his arms captured her and he kissed her back gave her a delicious shiver.

The faerie realm still slept, she could feel the light soul bodies slumbering all around her. She had fallen asleep in the ferns by the lake. But now Lilja tensed as thoughts of Grey gave way to her present worries.

Peri had promised to meet her so that she could go back to see Grey and the horses, but the day had gone and Peri had not arrived. Lilja tried to be brave and not cry, but several times a tear or two had crept down her cheeks. Faeries were supposed to be a happy lot, but she felt nothing close to happy of late. She was terribly worried about dear friend, and she kept thinking there was something she had forgotten. Or someone. But how could she forget another faerie? It was unheard of in this mystical world. Peri would never break a promise made, and Lilja began to wonder if something terrible might have befallen her friend. She had debated what to do all day and half the night, before she'd fallen into a restless sleep.

Her previous return to the faerie realm had been just in the nick of time. Peri had been waiting for her at the lake bottom and they had surfaced quickly. Peri had been shocked when she saw that Lilja was naked, but Lilja had quickly materialized dry garments and they'd run to the glen to dance in the light of the fireflies. As far as she knew, no one had noticed their late arrival as they danced blissfully under the moon. Even so, Lilja felt conflicted by her deceit. Peri assured her other faeries didn't know the portals had been sealed, but Lilja thought otherwise. She felt their curiosity. They didn't understand her fascination with the humans. Even she did not understand it, but she knew she wanted to visit Grey again and she wanted to understand him. There were possible repercussions for her each time she returned, but that didn't worry her as much as the possibility that her lack of concern might have placed her friend in jeopardy.

As Lilja listened to the enchanted animals of the forest chatter quietly, she wondered if she dared go to the bottom of the lake by herself. The thought terrified her.

Sitting up, brushing the hair back from her face, she saw the bandage Grey had placed on her cut finger. She unwound it now, carefully examining the finger to find it completely healed.

Feeling almost disgruntled, for even this small reminder of their time together had been erased, she rose and moved silently over to a small silvery portal at the entrance to the woods. Experimentally, she brushed her hand over the portal's smooth, glasslike surface, thinking of Grey and his ranch. It wobbled slightly but did not open. She tried again, and this time she grew excited to see the blue sky, the hills, and the horses running outside in the fresh new snow.

"Grey," she said softly, zeroing in on him as he stood looking up, almost into her face, but she knew he could not see her. She brushed her hand over the portal and tried to put her hand through it, but there was a resistance she couldn't penetrate.

The portal wobbled and went dark, erasing all she had seen. She sat down on a moss-covered log, disheartened. Would Grey forget about her? After all, many humans had forgotten a long time ago that faeries existed. They believed in them as children and then they grew up into non-believers.

Why would he have reason to remember her, except for the fact she had made his horses well? She was a common faerie here in the realm. There were many faeries more beautiful and more skilled. Unlike many other faeries, her talents were rarely called upon in her world. She knew of the importance of her skills, but she also knew they would be more highly prized outside her own homeland.

Lilja pulled her legs up and rested her chin on her knees. Scarlet fireflies with gossamer thin gold wings flitted around her head and then in front of her face. They were so happy here in their own environment; why could she not be happy and content where she belonged? Why must she yearn after a human?

Lilja tightened her mouth. She admitted it. Healing was her calling, but it was Grey she really wanted to see, to touch. After all, she had cared about him a very long time and only now was she suspecting it was something much deeper than she'd realized, something she had never experienced before. Why else did her heart ache and her mind return again and again to their time together?

She moved to the water's edge, and softly she began to sing in hopes of washing away the ache that coiled inside. As daylight broke, Lilja moved quietly through the realm. As Peri's absence grew longer, she feared something was dreadfully amiss. Her dear friend would surely have come to her if nothing was wrong.

She searched Peri's dwelling and all her favorite spots along the glen but was unable to find her. Lilja made her way into the university building, and it was there she came upon Lukais. He was perusing some heavy tomes in the library and looked up as she approached. He smiled to see her and she recalled the times growing up when she had found him in much the same place, reading ancient faerie history. Many times she had joined him and become absorbed in the rich lore.

But now, Lilja felt little peace in thinking about history. She felt too unsettled by Peri's absence.

"Good morning," she greeted the high elder.

"Fair morning to you," said Lukais, a fond grin curling his lips.

"I have an urgent matter I wish to bring before the high elder council," she blurted, unable to quell the urgency riding her. "My dear friend Peri is missing. I have called for her in all her favorite places, but she does not answer. She cannot be found."

Lukais closed the large book and his face grew thoughtful. "Lilja, think on this matter. Recall when I cautioned you against your interest in the earth realm -- but you would not listen," he said.

Dread tightened the back of her throat. "What do you mean?"

"You pulled your friend Peri into your preoccupation with the humans, against our advice and against the council's wishes."

"What harm has any of this done? Why are you so set against my studying the humans?"

"Is that all it is?" he asked. "A study? I think you will admit it goes further than that. I fear you are leaving us."

"And what if I do? Surely it is my choice to go where my skills will be of benefit? Aisywel is my homeland, I would always return here."

"Lilja, you are fortunate to live in our glorious faerie realm. Do you know what a human would sacrifice to have this eternal life?"

Lilja turned away, frustrated by his inability to understand. "I need to find Peri," she said distractedly. "Something terrible has happened."

"You will not find her this day," he said. She had never heard such a stern voice from him before.

Her heart grew cold. "What do you mean?"

"The council sensed her involvement and her sympathy for your preoccupation. She has been sent to another district."

Lilja's heart snapped and broke. "You have banished her from the home she loved?"

"Merely a temporary leave of absence until she understands the harm that could befall both of you in continuing on this course."

"You must bring her back! You cannot punish her for what I have done. This is her home. She will be heartbroken."

"Contrary to what you may believe, the high elder council acted for the benefit of both of you. Peri has been given a new assignment and seems quite happy in that situation. When the time is right, she will be allowed to come back and can once more situate herself among the Aisywel faeries. If you recall, she is not of this realm and had been merely visiting here at length."

Lilja's heartbeat slowed a bit.

"It is not a punishment," he said gently. "All Peri knows is that she has a new assignment."

Lilja frowned. "She never told me she was only here on assignment."

The high elder shrugged. "You know Peri has a soul gift for painting the true heart of her subjects, and you no doubt saw her beautiful art of faerie life here. She was invited here to record our life in paintings."

"Yes, of course."

"Lilja, Peri was a new friend for you, but friends sometimes move on to accomplish other goals in their lives. At any rate, what is necessary has been done," he said with finality. "It is out of my hands."

"And what about me?" she asked, feeling a trace of belligerence, "I am the one who began this quest to visit the earth realm. Will you send me elsewhere? Maybe banish me to some dark hillock so the mad trolls of Mortog will dance on my head?"

"No Lilja. I fear you would cause disruptions in other realms, even among the crazed trolls. You will stay here and reflect upon your life as a good faerie. So many heartbeats of time you have studied diligently, aiding our society with your gifts. I would hope you will see the wisdom in returning to such studies." He indicated the book before him. "We can begin right now."

"I feel unable to do so," Lilja said. Sadly, she added, "Can't you understand how badly I feel over the loss of my friend? It feels unjust that she would be sent away."

"We make decisions that protect all faeries."

Lilja felt an uncustomary anger rise inside her. "Well, apparently I am the worst faerie Aisywel has produced!" she cried, angered by his complacency. She spun on her heel and ran across the room but turned back at the doorway. "And I am glad, do you hear me? I am glad!"

"The portals are rechecked regularly," his voice carried after her. "You will not find a way out again. I hope in time you will see the council's wisdom in keeping you safe."

Frustrated and fearful, Lilja ran all the way back to the lake. The sun came up fully in the sky as her chest burst in sorrow. Deep anguish filled her. Peri was gone. Aisywel no longer felt like the same enchanted place of her birth. Her thoughts turned dark. How had this happened? Was it so terrible her visits to the earth dimension?

Lilja looked inward, grasping at a memory. The name came to her again, teasing. *Pandimora. She needed to know Pandimora's story!*

For once she did not see the little sprites playing at the forest's edge, or the dragonflies zinging about, trying to engage her in a game of hide and seek. Little bubbles of gold and silver light floated in the air, but all she felt was a terrible weight. Peri had been banished because of her. If she was gone, would they let Peri come home? She stared out across the water, fear tightening her chest until she thought it would drown her. And what about Pandimora? How would she find information on a faerie no one remembered?

"Can I find my way through the portal?"

Shaking, taking a deep breath to still some of the fear in her heart, Lilja searched the edges of the lake and finally found what she was looking for. A large Amazonian water lily. It would easily accommodate her weight so that she could float out to the middle of the lake. Gathering all her courage, she found a large round stone to bring her to the bottom when she reached the deepest part of the lake. With the stone in her arms, she climbed onto the water lily, careful not to let the stone break through the brilliant green skin of the lily pad. As if she were merely interested in floating atop the translucent waters, she let the water lily drift her away to the heart of the lake.

***

Grey pushed himself up in bed, the dream he'd been having fading as he rubbed his eyes. Sweat chilled on his shoulders and chest. He'd dreamed of Lilja, but she'd been far out of his reach, deep down in the lake, floundering as she tried to get back.

Something or someone kept her from returning. He felt her all around him, filling him. In the dream she'd thrown a key at him and as he reached out to grab it, he fell into a deep green abyss.

"Swim," she'd said, but though he followed her voice as he'd fought his way to the gelatin-like surface, he couldn't find her. His heart was still pounding over the imagined struggle.

He leaned back against his headboard, putting his hands through his hair and then rubbing his face. He looked over at the bedside clock. Three a.m.

With a groan, Grey got out of bed, pulled on some jeans and walked out to the living room. He put a piece of wood on the fire then moved to stare out the front window at the fields outside. The moon rode high in the sky tonight, shining over the pristine white snow. He leaned a fist against the wall, seeing in his mind Lilja the last time she'd been with him.

He was driving himself crazy over this, but what could he do? His throat went dry. What if Lilja never came back? Or what if she drowned trying to get back?

He leaned down, peering through the window and out into the moon-washed night again. Had there been a blue tinted flash? Heart hammering, Grey yanked open the front door, the chill air hitting his chest. Adrenaline racing, he grabbed his boots and shoved his bare feet into them. Lacing them quickly, he grabbed his heavy jacket.

He ran out the door and down the steps, ignoring the icy needles of cold that hit his chest. He swore he saw something out on the snow. He ran across the packed snow path to where he'd marked the portal, grateful the moon was so bright.

He stopped at the portal area and again saw a small flash.

"Lilja!" She lay curled on the ground at his feet, unmoving.

With a grunt, Grey lifted her dead weight up and into his arms. A rock the size of a softball fell to the snow. Her wet dress quickly began to grow cold in the night air. If she'd been out here longer, she'd be frozen to the ground.

"Grey."

"You're safe," he said, hurrying back toward the house. Climbing the steps, he kicked the door closed and placed her on the couch by the fire. Her dress was plastered to her and already beginning to get stiff with ice. Unable to find any buttons or zips, he took out his knife and carefully cut the garment up the side, then pulled it from her arms. She lifted her hips so he could get the rest of it off her. Quickly, he wrapped her in his warm quilt. Her skin was pale as he checked her breathing.

Lilja took a deep breath, her chest expanding. Her eyes snapped open, startlingly black with barely a trace of green. She stared up at him sightlessly, a lingering trace of terror evident. She took another breath and began to cough. He held her close, and when the coughing subsided, he gently wiped her face with a small cloth.

With her eyes back to normal, Lilja managed a smile. Grey hugged her fiercely. At least now she was safe here with him.

Grey lifted her, quilt and all, and sat down with

her on the couch. Leaning back, he cradled her against him, rubbing her wet hair with a towel. He'd kept everything he'd need close by in case she came back. Fine tremors shook her, but her eyes remained closed. He checked her pulse and was glad to find her vitals appeared to be normal -- well, normal by human standards.

Grey re-tucked her arms into the warmth of the quilt, glad when her shaking gradually subsided and she lay still against him. Watching the flames in the stove, Grey gradually drifted to sleep, and a new contentment began to wind around him.

Lilja had returned to him.

∞ Chapter Eight ∞

Lilja kicked her legs wildly, trying to pull herself to the water's surface. Gasping in huge gulps of air, she began to flail her arms.

"Lilja. Lilja!" A hard band was around her arms, keeping her from flailing. She bucked against the band, but gradually the voice soothed her and she opened her eyes. Wildly, she looked around. Sunlight played across the room and she found Grey's brown eyes close to her own. She looked into his concerned face with wonder, relaxing into him, then frowned as she looked beyond his shoulder at the wood paneled walls.

"I'm at your home, Grey."

"Yeah," he said. "Relax, you're safe with me now."

And she did relax. "I was so cold." But now warmth permeated her to her very bones.

"You were cold and wet when I found you," he

said.

Grey sat up, and the loss of his arms around her made her sit up, too.

"Stay there," he cautioned. "Stay warm."

Grey stood, clad only in dark jeans, which rode low on his lean hips. As she watched, he grabbed a long-sleeved garment and pulled it over his head, covering the dusting of hair on his chest and then the sinewy muscles of his back.

"You look very strong," she observed. "Faeries are different."

"Is that a good thing?" he asked with a small grin. "Or rather, do you think it's a good thing?"

She smiled. "Yes. I find you very attractive." She frowned. "But how did I get here?" she chewed a corner of her lip, looking up at him.

He looked concerned. "You don't recall?"

She leaned back, clasping her knees as she pulled the quilt around her. She closed her eyes, shuddering. "The lake."

"We need to talk." His voice took on a grim quality now. "But you need to get dressed first. I'll be right back." He left the room, returning with an armful of garments. "These are more of my sister's clothes. Why don't you go in the bedroom and get dressed?"

Lilja gathered the quilt tightly to her body so she didn't trip and followed him to the bedroom. She sensed he needed to keep occupied right now; otherwise she would have just manifested clothes instantly.

When Grey closed the door, she stood a moment and looked around the light-colored wood walls.

Although sparse in comparison to her little cottage with its greenery and flowers, she liked the painted art on his walls depicting scenes of the mountains and hills around them.

The paintings stirred a deep ache in her heart as she thought again of her missing friend Peri and her soul gift. A large glass window filled one entire wall, and Lilja imagined that in the daylight, Grey could lie in bed and look out to the hills and beyond. She wondered if he made love in the sunlight as it streamed across his bed. With a sigh, Lilja dressed in the slim-fitting black jeans and fluffy pink sweater. Pink had always been her favorite color.

When Grey returned after a small rap on the door, she opened the door, stretching her arms over her head. She opened her mouth in a yawn and, eyes wide, laughed with delight. "We don't do that on Aisywel," she said. "That was very nice."

He gave a bark of laughter. "No yawns in Aisywel? You're probably exhausted. With everything you've said about Aisywel, it sounds like some kind of utopia. Life is happy and wonderful, not stressed out as life can be here."

She nodded. "That is an accurate description -- at least most of the time."

"Then why would you ever want to come here?" he asked curiously. "We're certainly far from an ideal society. Even the weather turns dark and gloomy at times, especially lately."

"Yes, and I fear the increasing unpredictability of your weather is a reflection of the unrest in our own world. But as I explained, I've always been curious about the emotional circumstances of this world."

She sat on the bed. "It's so curious to me how emotions can direct your lives."

"But sometimes emotions can lead to painful experiences."

Eyes wide, she nodded. "Yes, I've seen that at times."

"Emotions, feeling a connection to someone, brings you closer to that person, but it also leaves you vulnerable."

"I think I understand. Peri thought she had a soul connection with a new soul in Aisywel, Herrikus, but he left our world for another faerie. Peri was very sad," she said quietly.

Grey sighed then sat on the bed beside her, making the mattress dip her toward him. "Lilja, we have to talk about you coming here through the lake. I can't have you doing this."

She looked at him and bit her lip. "You don't want me to come anymore?"

He took a deep breath, his eyes deeply intent on hers. "I want you to stay here," he said. "I don't want you to leave, but I'm not sure I have the right to ask. Each time you leave, I'm afraid you'll drown."

"Grey, if I want to see you," she said, "it's the only way."

"Then stay," he said. "Don't go back."

"I can't stay," she said sadly. "If I never returned to Aisywel, I would lose my immortality."

"You never die? Wow. And I guess even with what's going on you would miss your home."

She shook her head quickly then met his gaze. "My friend Peri has been sent away because of me. They've sent her to another district. Peri -- who loved our faerie realm so very much. All she did was try to help me."

"What have they done to her?" he asked.

"I wasn't able to find her. We were supposed to meet yesterday at daybreak by the lake, but she never came. I searched everywhere for her, all her favorite places and nowhere was she found. When I went to the university to file an accounting, the elder Lukais told me the council had sent her on another assignment. And it's my fault." Lilja hung her head. "I'm the one who should be taken away, not Peri."

"Tell me what this means," Grey said urgently. "You've observed our world, what does it mean to go to another district? Is it like being taken to jail?"

"I'm not sure. I have heard talk of faeries being banished to a non-world. There is no singing, no dancing, and there will certainly be no swimming. I don't know if that's what happened with Peri, but the elder said she was on a new assignment." She pressed her lips together. "Peri is a very sensitive soul. She is gifted in truly understanding what is in a person's heart and her understanding flows into the drawings and paintings she creates." Lilja looked up at him, pushing back the wing of hair that hung over her eye. "The next district is strict and rather dark in nature. If she was sent there, I can't bear the thought."

"But it might be just as the elder said, that she's on a new assignment. Do you think they're trying to isolate you? And for what reason?"

Slowly she said, "There are never conflicts or arguments in my world. No dissent or discord."

"Until now. How do you know you won't be the next one to disappear?" His voice was grim. "How would I find you?"

"The elder Lukais said I would cause disruption wherever I went."

Grey paced the floor. "I don't like this. If you were told such a thing, how can you trust this elder? Maybe he's got his own plans."

Lilja shook her head.

Grey sat next to her. "Lilja, I'm a cop and I think like a cop. There's always a reason behind someone's actions or lack thereof. What is your relationship with this Lukais?"

"He has been a trusted elder of Aisywel for a long time -- one of the most revered of the elders. He is caretaker of the Aisywel crystals and his responsibility is to keep all the worlds on an even balance."

"Does he seem fair? Do you think he would ever say one thing and then secretly do another?"

She bowed her head.

His hand gently lifted her chin.

The corners of Lilja's eyes became damp. In wonder, she put her finger to the wetness. "I never thought so all my life," she admitted. "But his adamant refusal to let me come here, and then Peri is sent away. Everything I thought I knew has been shaken to the core. I am no longer certain what I can believe in my own world. And ... " she hesitated.

"And what?"

"I don't know. He was very unhappy when I mentioned Pandimora. In my heart there is a worry over this faerie, yet I can't recall her history."

"Did she leave or run away?"

"I don't know."

"And what of your parents and family?" he asked. "Won't they be worried about you?"

"We are raised in a community with all the children together. The elders of the community raise us with their vast knowledge. We are shown all the facets of living: compassion, trust, survival, kindness. Our training is completed at what you would consider a young age. When faeries are ready, the elders identify each child's special abilities, what we call a soul gift, and their talent is melded to their soul."

"I'm assuming you were found to have healing skills?"

"Yes. We are encouraged to develop our individual skills."

"Do you have a choice?"

"Of course." But she frowned, remembering something from a long ago memory.

"Does anyone ever reject the talent they're melded with?" he asked.

"There is a vague memory -- we children were not supposed to know, but I do recall something, a story of a young male faerie who vehemently rejected his soul gift."

"What happened?"

"They made him keep the skill and melded it to his soul."

"Doesn't sound like a happy faerie to me. Do you recall his skill?"

"He was a seeker of truth and he would hear the heart's truth behind the words and actions. But there are some truths a child should not have to witness. He refused to use his soul gift."

"I know you said this is a happy place, Lilja, but I'm developing a little different mindset here from everything you've said."

She nodded. "It does appear many things have been hidden. Perhaps I have been afraid to examine them too closely."

"And there is no mother or father in Aisywel?"

"No. Many times they go off to other realms. I am not sure why." She reached out and touched his arm because it brought her great comfort to do so. "I often wondered what it would be like to grow up in a family as I have observed in your world. Like your family, Grey." She saw the question in his eyes. "Do you remember the little girl you used to play with when you went to the meadow behind your house?"

Grey frowned at her.

"When you were a small child," she coaxed.

He narrowed his eyes at her. "How --? But she moved away," he finally said.

She shook her head. "No, Grey, you moved away from believing. When you no longer believed, I no longer existed."

Grey looked stunned. "You were that child?"

Lilja nodded. He reached out to her and gently stroked the hair from her forehead, cupping her cheek with his hand. "That was a long time ago. I remember when we used to play." He tightened his lips. "I'm sorry I forgot," he said. "I believe in you now, Lilja, though I had moments where I wondered if I was crazy. I don't want you to leave." He pulled back. "Maybe if you talk to the elders --"

"No, Lukais has spoken. They are very staunch on this. They closed all the portals, except of course for the lake portal. Peri thought it was an ancient portal that had been lost to time, older even then the elders."

"How long is that?"

"Possibly three thousand or more human years." She shrugged. "I am not certain of time in human years."

"How old are the elders?" She sensed his deep curiosity coupled with amazement.

"Lukais is over nine hundred years old, the elder Bernate is six hundred and seventy-five, while Matlei is only five hundred and thirty years."

Grey looked rather stunned as he grappled with information that had to be very strange to him.

"And you, Lilja, how old are you in human years?"

"I am only two hundred and three in the faerie realm," she said. "In your human years, I am about twenty-eight years." She gripped his hands. "Do you see my dilemma, Grey? They might not know of that portal. That's why Peri and I had to be very secretive. If they discover its existence, I will never be able to come."

"But every time you go in the water --"

"But if it's the only way --"

"No, you can't risk it."

"There is no other way. They have closed their hearts to reason."

"There must be a safer solution," he said, his voice strong with determination. "Maybe I can go with you, make sure you make it out safely, then I can come back home."

The generosity of his offer touched her deeply, but she shook her head. "You don't understand what you'd be risking," she said. "I appreciate your offer, but it's not possible. If you were caught, you would be seized and held in a suspended state while the high tribunal decided if you were a threat. Time moves different in my home than here on the earth dimension. You could lose an entire month of your time." She snapped her fingers. "Just like that."

His concern wound around her and she began to identify what was in her heart. The feelings blossomed deeply, the burgeoning love and respect she felt for him crystal clear and wonderfully exhilarating. Yet pain also grew. How could love flourish for them between their two worlds? They were both firmly entrenched in their separate lives.

She placed her hand over his heart, the connection giving rise to blue sparks. "No longer a fractured soul," she said softly. "Your heart now beats true and in tune with your life." Vibrant. "You have healed yourself and are whole once more."

"You've helped me," he said, gripping her fingers. "Just as you healed my animals."

She smiled. "Grey, healing is always a soul's choice."

"Caring about you has made it easier for me to see what I was missing."

She leaned against his shoulder, basking in the warmth and caring she felt for this man.

"I always wondered how humans managed to filter through the multitude of emotions your world is privy to. Since I have known you, Grey, I have begun to understand the complexity of this journey, walking in emotion."

"And what emotions have you discovered, Lilja?"

"Joy in my heart when I am with you," she said, staring into his brown eyes. "Joy of course is well known in the faerie realm. We live with it daily and have really never known anything else. But this type of joy here," she pointed at her heart, "is something I have never experienced. It is so expansive."

"Trust me, I understand, sweetheart," he said. "I'm happier than I've been in a long time since you showed up, though I have to admit it's a bit mind-boggling to realize you're not human but from a hidden world."

"There is no fear and no dark emotions. We know of them in other places and vibrations, but not in Aisywel -- well, we were insulated from that knowledge." She frowned. "But of late, I am out of sync with my dear Aisywel. I feel disharmony there, in myself and with the decisions the council has made. I even raised my voice to the elder," she whispered. "I was so angry."

"How do other faeries feel about what is happening there?" he asked curiously.

"That is what I find interesting. They seem oblivious to the changes. However, I do notice the pace of life in Aisywel seems to have shifted, as if faeries are more rushed in their duties. I don't understand it."

"Did you ever consider that maybe you've grown distant from their way of life because of your travel here?"

"Yes, of course. And I believe that is why the

council wants my activity restricted. Perhaps they fear my actions will cause others to be curious about life outside Aisywel. If faeries began to leave our realm in numbers, it would endanger the existence of our world."

"We need to come up with a solution," Grey said. "I want to make sure you're safe, but it's up to you to choose where you want to be." He dipped his head and kissed her cheek, but then she turned her head, wanting to feel his mouth on hers.

"Kiss me again, Grey. It gives me such a wonderful feeling."

"I'll second that," he said, and pulled her forward into his arms, leisurely kissing her from her chin to her forehead. Lilja felt a deep ache in her stomach, and she moved restlessly against him, capturing his mouth with her own. The touch of his tongue upon her lips felt glorious. Her heart swelled as her energy merged with his.

He kissed her deeply again but then pulled back slightly. "Um, sweetheart, it feels like that light is engulfing us."

Lilja opened her eyes. "Grey, there is no need for concern. Our merging energies are dancing with joy."

"The same energy you use to heal the animals," he said, amazed.

"This life force fuels every living thing. As emotions engage and deepen, so too will the intensity of the light."

Lilja sat on the bed, her eyes on Grey. Slowly, she pulled the pink sweater over her head, folded it neatly and then pushed the black jeans down her legs. She stared at him, aware of his heart reaching out to her.

She grabbed the bottom of Grey's shirt and pulled it up over his head, enjoying the sight of his muscled chest. She smiled at him, bringing his palms to her breasts while her hands roamed in exploration over his chest. Fire merged with emotion, burning, as the light swirled around them.

"I want to be closer to you, Grey," she murmured, registering her own deepening breath, her heart beating quickly, the back of her neck growing damp.

His hands were heated brands on her flesh and she pressed up against him. "I would like to make love with you, Grey, so I can fully experience such a bonding. Surely making love is the deepest expression of emotion!"

"Lilja, I want to make love to you more than anything right now, but be sure about this. There's no going back once it happens. I mean, is it okay -- a faerie and a human?"

She gave a small gurgle of laughter. "Despite the elders trying to keep the faeries contained, our people have been intermingling for a long time." She looked all around them. "Look at the light around us -- the energy of our souls has already merged and interchanged. The physical act of love will further bring us together in a merging of energy. It's surely the only way to fully appreciate the emotions that dance between us."

He shook his head slightly. "Let's hope we don't burn up."

"No, Grey! We'll be exploring the mystical reactions we have to each other."

His mouth moved over hers, slow and tantalizing, the texture curious to her. She pressed her fingers to his lips, a man hard in body and yet with lips provocatively soft and knowledgeable. His mouth moved down to her breasts, his tongue creating such heat she felt as if her skin had truly been touched by lightning. Her body gave a small involuntary jerk and she inhaled deeply, caught off guard by a multitude of new sensations. She had the strangest sensation she wanted to jump out of her skin and dance for joy.

Lilja ran her hands down over Grey's body, and he rolled over so that now she was on her back with him above her. She felt immense power as his heart reached out to hers. She savored each sensation, knowing a communication from heart to heart and deep into the soul was not to be rushed. She touched the pads of her fingers to his chest, traced the muscled contours, the light sprinkling of dark brown hair, followed its path as it wound down to his flat belly.

Grey reached into a table beside the bed, and Lilja watched curiously as he grabbed a small packet.

"Grey, what is that?"

He smiled. "A condom. I don't want to take a chance that I could get you pregnant."

She nodded. "Of course you are right to think of that. Being so close to the earth, faeries are very fertile. But unlike with human chemistry, a faerie consciously decides if she will become pregnant."

He paused a moment after tearing the packet open, taking a deep breath, his brown eyes looking directly into her. "You're sure about this?"

"Yes."

Grey lowered his body to her and she opened her legs as he gently ran a hand down over her hip and thigh, moving her knee back. He pressed his tongue to her lower lip and then into her mouth as he entered her body.

Lilja became fully aware of the blood rushing throughout her body, her heart pumping quickly, her head lolling back on the pillows, her fingers gripping his hips. The sensation of joining with Grey was an experience she had never imagined for herself. She could feel her soul expanding and reaching out to Grey to gently enfold him, then the rush of blood and adrenaline carried her along, quickening her heart.

Lilja began to shake. So many sensations, so much bombardment of nerve endings clamoring for release, muscles contracting, synapses sending out signals, connecting with cells and creating a screaming sensation along her entire body. Her breath came fast and when he hesitated, she pulled his hips down and pressed up onto him. Her spine curved, her body supple and giving, taking, as he gave and took away.

"Lilja ..." He kissed her, his body thrusting in and out of her own, the fit perfect, light exploding all around them as he entered her fully and Lilja thought she would surely shatter into a million pieces of faerie dust. She tried to move closer and deeper to him, feeling his body connecting with her innermost recesses. Such an explosion of colors behind her lids as she momentarily closed them, just concentrating and fully immersing herself in the feel of Grey's body within her own. She encouraged him to move faster, feeling as if the world was closing in around just the two of them. She tightened all her muscles, throwing her head back, tensing as endorphins rushed through every portion of her body, feeling as if Grey were touching every part of her.

And as she shattered with Grey's arms around her, she felt the breaking apart of their souls, and then the merging together, and for a moment in time there was no distinction where human began and faerie left off. They became as one.

"Hold me tightly," she whispered.

She could feel his smile against her cheek. "I am."

"Tighter," she said.

And as they both moved into an explosion of light and sensation, they were showered with miniscule particles of faerie dust. A gust of air coiled around them, but they held tightly to each other, and eventually the air became calm and all settled down once again. The blue strings of light zigzagged wildly about their heads and naked bodies, until eventually it subsided and their heartbeats also slowed.

***

Grey didn't care if he ever moved. Everything around him and Lilja still pulsed, the bed sheets beneath them vibrating slightly as if holding the memory of their lovemaking. He shook his head, trying to assimilate the experience of making love with Lilja. Other worldly.

She pressed kisses along his jaw and down the side of his neck. "You've surely turned my world upside down," he said as she lay in the hollow of his arm. His thumb caressed the back of her hand and up to her wrist. He let out a long breath. "That light almost blinded me," he said.

"It was intense," she agreed, one brow lifted. She began to laugh. "Grey, I expect you will get used to it in time. That is the difference between our worlds. My ancestors have always celebrated intense interactions with bursts of light and the play of energy."

He squeezed her closer to him. "Sweetheart, that was more than a burst of light. Are you feeling okay?"

"I am feeling very happy." She rolled over onto his chest as an all-body shiver moved through her. "And yes, I am still feeling aftershocks." She gurgled with laughter and he traced the smooth skin of her back and down over her hips. A part of him that had been empty for a long time now felt curiously different, and it was good. He liked being able to laugh again. A woman in his arms who made him feel something different ... more alive.

He pulled her with him as he lay back on the sheets. "My brave little faerie dared to shake me out of my solitary existence," he said.

"And you have shown me the truth about experiencing an emotional connection," she said quietly. "Someday I hope to show you a true faerie soul connection."

He lifted his brow. "You mean there's more?"

"Much more."

***

Lilja stirred, having enjoyed a sweet nap in

Grey's arms. She felt content to lie here, but knew there were questions she must ask. "Can you tell me about Annie?" Lilja asked. She felt him stiffen slightly, but it was important for her to know why he suffered over her death.

"It was three years ago, Lilja." After a moment, he said. "Annie was a strong woman, but that day she took an unnecessary risk, riding out on Raven after a storm. She was a photographer and was determined to take pictures of the river after a spectacular rainfall. She was six months pregnant. When the horse fell in the slick footing, she lay in the mud for hours before I got home. Raven was waiting for me when I pulled in from work. When I saw her standing in the driveway, her legs bleeding, I knew something terrible had happened.

"If I'd been home," he added harshly, "I could have prevented her from going out."

Lilja touched his cheek with a gentle hand. "Grey, do you really believe you could have prevented her from doing what she wished?"

He put his head back. "Annie had a mind of her own."

"And she had safely ridden many times without harm."

"True."

"As much as it hurts, sometimes things happen just as they are meant to. Humans follow the passion in their hearts." Slowly, she said, "It always puzzled me why some will take chances without knowing the outcome. Understanding has grown in me that if your heart feels something deeply, you follow your bliss without thought for consequences."

"But at times risks can be taken to foolish heights."

"I am sorry for the loss you have suffered, Grey. Human souls create a birth plan before they arrive in this dimension," she added slowly, thoughtfully. "As difficult as it might be for you to believe, all three of you were at that planning meeting of souls."

Grey shook his head. "This is too much." He moved to the edge of the bed, then he stood, grabbing his jeans and quickly yanking them up. He buckled his belt and grabbed a short-sleeved shirt, his movements jerky as he walked across the room.

Lilja knew he needed time to absorb what she had told him. There were still residues of anger tightly coiled inside him.

He paused in the doorway, the shirt clenched in his fist. "I'll get us something to eat."

***

Lilja dressed in the clothes Grey had provided. Her body still resonated with the energy of their lovemaking, her skin sensitive as her thoughts lingered on him. She ran her fingertips along her arm, remembering Grey's fingers taking the same path. She hugged herself. He was a good man, caring for his animals with patience, trying to move forward in his life despite the pain of the past.

With a sigh, Lilja walked toward the kitchen. She watched Grey as he moved to the big white freezer container against the wall. He moved effortlessly, a man physically strong and assured in his world. He turned to look at her as he opened cupboards on the wall.

She studied him, understanding a little of the

pain he must be experiencing. To lose a loved one felt as if part of the heart had been ripped away. Lilja wasn't sure how she knew that, but that thought resonated with her.

Grey looked down at two bowls he'd placed on the counter. "I'll have this ready in a minute if you want to relax by the warm fire."

"That sounds wonderful." She nodded, understanding he wasn't able to talk about Annie and the child just yet.

Before she exited the kitchen, his voice came to her gruffly. "Do you know if Annie suffered?"

"No. Their souls crossed over swiftly."

"How do you know?"

"We of the fae can see when a soul moves into a dimension of light."

"Thank you."

She exited the kitchen and walked back into the cozy living room. Sitting before the fire, Lilja stared at the leaping flames. She thought of the horses in the barn and opened a small portal to touch and soothe them. She crooned a soft, sweet song to complete their healing, stroking Raven's silky nose then rubbing the white star on Dancer's forehead.

"Perhaps one day I will stay here with you, dear hearts," she murmured to them softly.

"That is not possible Lilja. You are to come with me."

Shocked, Lilja spun quickly to see the elder Lukais. He stood in a portal in the wall right next to her chair.

The wood wavered, the molecules displaced, and the opening shimmered with a silver light.

Imperiously, he held out his hand.

With some trepidation, Lilja folded her arms and pushed herself deeper into the chair. "I will not come. I will not return where faeries are treated with so little respect."

He stepped fully into the room, white brows raised, then spread his arms wide and declared, "This is what you would trade for our enchanted world? A semblance of nature -- emotional turbulence, instability. *Mortality*."

"I am staying." She steeled herself to meet the elder's gaze.

His blue eyes were piercing. "You have always been a favorite, Lilja, a studious pupil. I believe you need time to adjust your thinking and fully realize what your refusal may cost you. I have given this matter great consideration. Come willingly with me and it will be a simple matter to allow Peripaus to return," he said softly.

Lilja caught her breath. "She can return to Aisywel?"

His eyes flickered with light. "If you come back to where you belong." He grabbed her arm.

Lilja felt the shock of his touch through her body. Light shot from his eyes and she instinctively ducked her head. Pain lanced her and she squeezed her eyes closed. Images flashed lightning fast behind her lids; her lifetime and heartbeats in images.

Shaken, she opened her eyes. "Where is my sister? What have you done to Pandimora?"

∞ Chapter Nine ∞

"Get away from her!" Grey snapped. He dropped the bowls he held onto a small table and reached for the rifle against the wall. He pointed it at the old man with the long white beard and robes. The man twisted his head around at an unnatural angle, twin points of light flaring in his eyes. Grey barely had time to register an uneasy shiver before the old man and Lilja were sucked back into the wall.

Grey lunged forward, reaching for her. He pulled back as the wall closed with a snap, catching his fingertips. He pushed against the now solid wall, leaving spots of blood with his torn fingers.

"Lilja!" He hit the wood with his fist, staring in disbelief and anger. They'd taken her. How could he fight beings he couldn't see in a world that was closed to him? He could have protected her if he hadn't been messing around in the kitchen.

Grey turned, catching his foot on one of the

ceramic bowls that had fallen to the wood floor. Strewn against the wall were blueberries, strawberries and raspberries from the freezer that he'd drizzled with honey. He closed his eyes. He'd prepared that treat in hopes of making up to her for his gruff behavior. He had planned to tell her how special she was to him and how much their time together meant to him.

"How do I get her back? How can I even track her down?" He pressed his clenched fist against the wall then leaned his forehead on his arm. Where could he find her? The horses.

Grey pulled on a pair of boots, yanked open the front door, barely hit the steps and raced to the barn. His heart hammered, hoping he'd find her out there. Maybe she could get away from the elder.

Grey opened the barn door and ran inside. "Lilja?" He checked the stalls. The horses stopped eating their hay to look at him. He probably looked like a crazy man as he searched for her.

He leaned back against Dancer's stall, his breath ragged as he looked around. He was a cop, he should know what to do. Except that he didn't. This was totally out of his realm of experience. Was it Lukais who had taken her? How did he get her back? What would they do to her for disobeying?

He heard his name being called. Heart leaping in hope, Grey ran outside again then slowed to a walk, surprised to see his brother again with a woman beside him. She had flaming red hair in a thick braid and barely reached Drew's shoulder. She was enveloped in Drew's coat.

"Grey, what's going on?" Drew asked, clearly

alarmed. "We saw you running around like a wild man."

Weary, Grey nodded at them and indicated the house. "Let's go inside. This may take awhile."

Inside the living room, Drew said, "Grey, you mentioned a woman, Lilja, when I was here earlier. This is Pandimora, Lilja's sister."

Shock rippled through Grey. He looked at his brother and then the petite woman. She smiled, her eyes similar in color to Lilja's, a deep sparkling blue-green.

He looked at his brother. "You know she's a --" he hesitated, searching Drew's face.

"A faerie," Drew said.

"You know," Grey said hoarsely. He sat down with a thump on the couch arm. "Geez."

"Grey, I'm pleased to meet you," said Pandimora. "Please understand I have been searching for my sister so I'm anxious to see her."

He read the excitement in her eyes and hated to extinguish it. "She's gone."

Pandimora gave a cry and dropped to sit on the couch.

Grey cleared his throat. "She told me she didn't have family."

Drew moved to sit beside Pandimora, placing an arm around her shoulders.

"I was afraid of this. She's been mind washed," Pandimora whispered.

Grey stared. "What?"

"Her memory erased," Drew said.

"The elder opened a portal and pulled her into the wall."

Pandimora now looked ready to cry.

"I tried to stop him --"

"Trust me, you can't fight him," Drew said grimly.

Grey snapped his head up. "How do you know?"

"We've been battling him all week." Drew looked at Pandimora. "Actually, probably longer. The time differences still confuse me."

Pandimora turned to Grey, took his hands in her own and examined his bleeding fingertips.

"They're fine," he said dismissively, pulling back.

She gripped his wrists with steely strength then blew gently on his fingers. Grey watched in amazement as the skin healed over, leaving only small white scars.

"What the heck?" He looked at her. "I guess I shouldn't be surprised. Lilja healed my horses."

Pandimora nodded. "All faeries have some healing skills, but Lilja's soul gift for healing is tremendous."

Grey looked at his brother.

"Briefly," Drew said. "Pandimora and Lilja are from the faerie realm Aisywel, a dimension hidden from most humans. Pandimora witnessed the elder Lukais hurt someone and before he could harm her, she managed to escape. I was driving outside of town through Dell's Bridge on an investigation when I found her in the road gravely injured. The rest has been an incredible time of alternate universes and faeries, goblins and bad tempered elders."

Grey looked at his brother. "I'm out of words." He stared at Pandimora, concerned. "Where would he take Lilja?"

"Aisywel."

"Can we get her back?"

Drew and Pandimora exchanged glances. "What don't I know?" A new tightness grew in Grey's chest.

Pandimora held out her arm so Grey could see a multi-pointed star tattoo on her arm.

"I am marked and banned from returning to Aisywel, and yet this elven star also offers protection. Lilja also has a mark, but hers is on her shoulder. The marks were bestowed upon us by our mother Clare before she disappeared many heartbeats ago. I had hoped Lilja would be safe since she has always been a favorite of the elder."

Grey looked at them with concern. "The council sent her friend Peri away because she helped her come here to heal my horses."

Pandimora's mouth thinned. "I suspect the council doesn't know any of this. I think it is all Lukais."

"I'm not surprised." Grey frowned. "Apparently her friend Peri found an old portal at the bottom of a lake." He shook off a shiver. "The guy that took her had white hair, beard and clothes. And a weird pinpoint of light in his eyes."

"Lukais," Pandimora said.

"What will he do to her?" Grey asked.

She avoided the question. "Show me where the portal manifested."

Grey indicated the now solid wall in his living room.

She put her hands to the wood siding, as if testing its firmness. Slowly, she said, "A new portal was created."

Puzzled, Grey stared at the wall.

"There are portals that have been in place for thousands of years," she explained. "This however, feels fairly recent."

"What does that mean?"

"Such a new portal can only be created by an elder. It is not easily detected and there would be no evidence he ever left Aisywel."

Grey's mouth went dry. "He could come and go as he pleased without anyone knowing."

Pandimora nodded, obviously distressed. Her eyes turned black with no trace of iris color. Grey looked at his brother, who stared at Pandimora.

"Where is the lake portal?" she asked.

"Outside."

Drew touched Pandimora's arm, enfolded her palm in his own. Grey saw the blue sparks of electricity curling around their joined hands.

"Can I get her back?" Grey asked.

"You will have to go after her," Pandimora said. Grey was relieved to see her eyes were back to normal. "You can get in to Aisywel, but whether you can leave -- it's extremely dangerous, Grey, and if you're caught --"

He grabbed his jacket. Opening the front door, he stepped outside.

"Grey!" she called.

He looked back.

"I'll walk with you. You'll need some preparation to enter the faerie realm."

***

Grey tested the faint blue portal with the toe of

his boot. It wobbled and gave like gelatin. He looked at Drew, standing there with his arm around Pandimora. He could see how much they cared for each other. He felt the same way about Lilja.

"Don't swim down," Pandimora said tersely. "Swim up as soon as your head is immersed. Remember, the worlds are reversed. If Lilja still lives in our little cottage, there is a path from the lake that will be lined with silver foxgloves. Lukais may have her imprisoned there or may be holding her elsewhere. If she is not at the cottage, there is a path straight out the back door leading into a dance circle in the forest. That is your last opportunity to find her. If she is not there you must retrace your steps and return. Follow only that path or you could be taken over by the enchantment of the dusk faeries. If that occurs, even Lilja will not be able to retrieve your soul."

"My soul?" Grey shook that off, not really wanting to think about it. He had to find her. Pandimora had given him a crash course in faeries and his head was still reeling. Who would believe a down-to-earth cop would be thinking about chasing down faeries? Or at least one faerie. Even more astonishing, Pandimora had mentioned they also had a brother who was missing. They had been mind washed to forget each other and none of them knew why. Pandimora had not known the whereabouts of the rest of their family.

Pandimora looked up at the sky as the afternoon sun waned. "We must wait until the sun goes down. It must be dusk in Aisywel."

"I'll take care of the horses until you get back,"

Drew said. "And for God's sake be careful."

If he made it back.

He read the worry in Pandimora's eyes.

"I'll find her," he promised.

"There is growing unrest in Aisywel -- anything can go wrong at any moment. The Deevs in the lower realm have begun coming through the gates and that will pose an added risk. Until the Deevs are stabilized and integrated, you must avoid them at all costs. For that reason also you must not deviate from the path I described."

"How will I know a Deevs?" he asked.

"You won't."

He lifted a brow.

"Avoid all life forms," she instructed. "That's why it's better to go at night. The faeries will be dancing and other life forms slumbering."

"How did you get in if you were banished?" Grey asked.

Drew said, "Pandimora made a bargain with two goblins to shift matter and sneak in." His brother grimaced. "Not something I recommend since it involves trusting a goblin to disassemble body molecules and cells one by one and reconstruct them on the other side."

"You too?" Grey asked, stunned.

Drew nodded then looked at Pandimora. "He won't run into goblins, will he?"

"I hope not." She sounded uncertain.

"If I find Lilja, will we be able to get out?" Grey wasn't going to worry about goblins.

"I hope so but it may be difficult since Lukais will have her under the crystals' surveillance. If you are caught, you must insist on being brought before the high elder council."

"What about the mark of protection on Lilja's shoulder? She never really mentioned it."

"She may not be aware of its significance. I didn't know myself about the significance of my elven star. As to what form of protection it may take, I can't tell you that either."

Uneasily, Drew said, "Maybe I should go with him."

Pandimora shook her head. "Lukais will have programmed the crystals to sense our presence if we re-entered Aisywel. We would have no chance." She looked up at the sky. "It's almost time."

Grey knew they were worried, but there were no assurances spoken and none expected. He hoped to make it back alive.

He shucked his heavy jacket, unlaced his boots and pulled them off along with his socks. Standing with his bare feet on top of his jacket on the snow, he took a deep breath and dropped into the portal.

∞ Chapter Ten ∞

Grey looked around the watery green depths then used his feet on the sandy bottom to propel himself upward. Colorful fish swam past him, but he ignored everything in his quest to reach the surface. He popped up like a cork, drawing in deep gulps of air, treading the incredibly buoyant water as he waited for his lungs to acclimate to the heavy, almost tropical air around him. In the near dusk, he saw the shore and swam for it. He was a good swimmer and felt in awe that Lilja, a non-swimmer, had had the courage to go into this lake. He had come up twenty feet or more from the bottom.

There was no way he was leaving here without her.

He walked from the water, his jeans and long-sleeved T-shirt shedding water with each step, the droplets looking like glints of gold as they dropped to the grassy shore. The air moved around him in swirling warm currents, and his clothing dried before he had taken four steps from the lake.

He shook his head in wonder then searched for the silver path Pandimora had told him to look for. Everything around him glowed with an almost iridescent green light, and as dusk deepened, he quickly located the growth of silvery foxglove bells which led into the heart of the woods. The ferns to his left shook and moved. Grey, his enforcement training deeply ingrained, felt the itch between his shoulder blades and knew he was under surveillance. He kept his gaze straight ahead and moved as quietly as possible.

No eye contact with any creatures, no matter how innocent or childlike in appearance. The sprites could carry you off and enchant you into playing hide and seek forever.

Grey followed the path. He hadn't had much time to process what she'd told him, but his focus remained razor sharp; Lilja's life depended on him following Pandimora's instructions to the letter.

What if Lukais had taken Lilja somewhere he couldn't find her? Somewhere even Pandimora wouldn't know?

An eerie shiver went up his spine as he looked around. He felt curiously out of sync and off balance. He just couldn't wrap his mind around the fact that a faerie world existed above them -- or below, he still wasn't clear on that point. He'd dropped into the portal but he'd swum up out of the lake.

Faeries, trolls ... what else existed just beyond the sight of most humans?

Grey finally emerged into a small clearing. In front of him was a tiny dwelling. It looked like something out of a child's fairy tale. Brown outer walls almost like gingerbread, rows of linked daisies carefully woven along a white picket fence. An abundance of flowers in colors he couldn't even identify sprang everywhere around the cottage. The flowers surrounding the cottage in such abundance appeared wilted until he entered the small white gate. Immediately, all the flowers snapped upright, as if standing to attention, their faces turned toward him, delicate stems waving gently as if stirred by a breeze. They seemed to be smiling at him. He moved carefully, keeping clear of any contact.

"Don't lose it now, Maddox," he muttered. He kept walking and felt a collective sigh in the air around him and then the chatter of muted voices. Something touched the back of his neck, but when he quickly turned, no one was there. He could have sworn it was the flowers talking as he proceeded quickly up the path toward the house.

When he reached the doorway, he pushed the door with two fingers. The long ferns at the entry way bowed down and caressed the tops of his bare feet. Careful not to step on them, he pushed the door open, ducking his head under the low archway as he entered.

"Lilja?" he called. The chatter behind him stopped. "Lilja?"

Even though it was dusk outside and he didn't see any lamps, the interior of the cottage glowed softly, as if waiting for her to return.

Although it was a simple, one-room cottage, he marveled at the intricately carved scrollwork along the windows and doorframe. The flowers and ferns that grew inside vined upwards to a ceiling skylight, and the stars twinkled brightly, closer than he'd ever seen in his life.

In the utter stillness, his uneasiness intensified. A chain of blue and white flowers draped over the door trim touched the top of his head, then his shoulder, and moved to trail down his back. Urging himself to remain calm, Grey carefully stepped sideways, mindful of his brother's words that the faeries had held him captive with a chain of daisies.

Pandimora had said if Lilja wasn't in her cottage, then he had to go to the glen. Around the back of the cottage he would find another path, this one lit by small blue glimmers of light. Grey reached to close the front door, but it slowly closed on its own. He walked through the cottage to the back door directly opposite the front door. With his imagination being stretched to capacity, he needed to stay focused. Everything he'd believed about reality was now turned upside down. There was no going back.

Once more outside, he found everything blanketed in a textured darkness, as if silk curtains hung around him, parting as he walked forward.

Grey fished in his jeans pocket and pulled out the small LED flashlight Pandimora had told him to bring. He pulled it from the plastic bag which had protected it from the water and stuffed the plastic back in his pocket. He would use the LED light only if necessary as it would be less detectable. He'd asked Pandimora if he had to be concerned with faeries being violent; it hadn't been reassuring that she'd been unable to answer his question.

Grey suddenly spotted the path of tiny

glimmering stars. Taking a deep breath, he followed the path deeper into dense woods but hadn't gone too far when he reached a clearing where a blazing fire had been lit. He couldn't believe his luck. Lilja sat beside the fire with her back to him. He'd recognize her anywhere, her dark glossy hair with its pink spiky wings shining by the light of the campfire.

Grey moved forward, relieved to find her so easily. "Lilja, I'm glad I found you. I've been worried like crazy." He touched her shoulder, but his hand went through her as she dissolved into fireflies that dispersed into tiny sparkles of light.

***

Lilja watched Grey walk into the trap and there was nothing she could do. The faeries danced in the glen under the light of the bright, bright moon and she doubted they were even aware of Grey's approach nor did she think Grey could see the enchanted faeries. The dance under the moon was usually a joyous exercise, but tonight Lukais had made it into a mockery and she wept inside at the loss of the glen's innocence.

Trapped in a silent, motionless void, she was unable to warn him. She watched his approach from the other side of the fire. Because they were on different vibrational planes, he could only see a mirror image of her.

The spell Lukais had woven held her immobile. It broke her heart into pieces to know her own kind would weave such an evil plot to keep her and Grey apart.

When Grey stepped into the ring of faerie grass

where her mirror image had been, she knew he was well and truly caught. Angry that he had been brought to this, she watched as he faded into nothing.

Lilja fought against the spell that bound her so tightly and heard the soft echo of laughter. Lukais.

He appeared before her in a shifting form. "Do not struggle, my dear Lilja. You will certainly bruise yourself." He stared at her with regret. "I can see your thoughts, Lilja, and you are incorrect: I have not succumbed to an evil demon. You do not know the meaning of evil. How could you, living in Aisywel? Why must you be contrary when all others abide by the order of our realm? Faeries have always enjoyed their warm days, beautiful haven and the most comfort anyone could wish for. They do not seek life outside Aisywel."

"Lukais, how can this happen? I remember how you guided me from a wee faerie, always sheltering me under your wisdom. What changed, Lukais?" For a moment she saw a remembrance of times past reflected in his eyes. Hope sprang inside her that something remained of that more compassionate Lukais.

He lifted a brow and the memories were extinguished. "Some actions, my dear Lilja, can never be undone." A trace of sadness colored his voice. "Words, once spoken, are forever captured by a tender heart. I made a choice a long time ago, and I am obliged to keep on that path." His face grew stern once more. "Promise me you will no longer seek the human world, and all this will be forgotten and washed away. You can go back to your life here in Aisywel."

"Forgotten?" Her heart beat faster. "Are you speaking of washing my memory -- again?" It frightened her to even say the words aloud, and when he simply looked at her, she knew she was right. "You have betrayed your responsibilities as a respected elder," she said, her voice trembling. "You are no more worthy of your position than the Deevs you would crush under your heel. Even now as the Deevs rush through the outer portals into Aisywel, you chase after me."

"Perhaps I should turn you over to them," he said, stroking his chin as if considering that option.

Terror filled Lilja.

With something like regret on his face, he lifted a hand, fingers spread wide, and from his hand dropped miniscule particles of red faerie dust. The dust encircled her, clinging to her aura as it pulled her away.

***

Grey inhaled several deep breaths as he felt himself solidify once more and looked down to see he was sitting on a chair. Talk about a freaked-out moment. He'd been standing, thinking he'd found Lilja in the clearing by the fire, and the next minute his body had dissolved into nothing. At least he could feel his feet again. He tried to lift his foot but found himself paralyzed. He craned his neck to look around as best he could, but he couldn't see Lilja anywhere.

The chair in which he sat was carved into what appeared to be reptile scales, and as he stared down at the chair it seemed to move slightly and change position. It almost felt as if it was ... alive. Warily, he puzzled why he couldn't move. He was not bound by any rope or wire, and yet he felt as if he were fast to the chair.

Grey's chair faced a long glass table that gently pulsed with red light. The room around him was enormous and made entirely of glass. He looked upward at the night sky. If the circumstances he was in hadn't felt so dire, he would have taken the time to marvel at the beauty of the stars above them. He frowned, snapping his attention away from the stars. He almost felt as if he was being pulled into a dreamy state of wonder.

The glass was domed and for the life of him he couldn't grasp how it was held together. It looked like one solid piece of glass, yet as Grey looked, he began to see that tiny sections of the glass were missing or broken. That in itself seemed strange to him in a world appearing so perfect.

Frustrated, Grey again tried to move his hands and arms. Three men entered the room in front of him. The first man was the old white bearded guy who'd grabbed Lilja at his place. Grey stiffened. *Lukais.* In his hand, the elder held an intricately carved wooden stick with green ivy vining along its length. Behind him were two younger men, one with close-cropped light blond hair and the other one with long black hair, both similarly dressed in long white robes. Grey hoped he wasn't in the faerie version of hell. Chairs materialized on the opposite side of the table and all three sat down facing him.

"Where is Lilja?" he demanded, surprised to find he could talk, even if he couldn't move.

The old man lifted a brow arrogantly then dipped his head to confer with the younger men, their voices low enough Grey couldn't make out the conversation.

Impatiently, Grey demanded, "I want to know what's going on. What have you done with Lilja and why are you keeping me glued to this chair?"

The three men looked at him in surprise, and then the old man stood. "We are the elders of Aisywel and this is our university hall. You will not speak unless we request you to do so."

"I suppose you're Lukais?" Grey said, earning himself a sharp look. "I have a right to know what's going on. I came looking for Lilja after you forced her to go with you."

"Lilja comes and goes as she pleases," he said placidly.

"Are you kidding?" Grey said derisively, "That's not how I saw it. There was no choice involved. You took her from my home forcefully."

Lukais looked at the other two elders and shrugged his shoulders. "That's absurd."

"Where is she?" Grey asked. He looked at the two other men. "Are you two also in on his crooked scheme?"

"You will show respect or I will silence your voice!" Lukais' wood stick struck the floor. For such a small stick, it made a thundering boom, rocking the floor under his chair and seeming to reverberate off the glass walls. "Do not fabricate human lies. This is a tribunal which will decide your fate for daring to invade the faerie realm."

Grey wondered if he was starting to rattle the

old man. "I'm stuck on this chair. The only thing I can do is ask questions. Is that what's scaring you -- that I might ask questions you don't want anyone else to hear?"

"You are insolent." Lukais looked back at the other elders. "But what can be expected of a human?" He turned back to Grey. "Tell me how you gained entry and I will return you unscathed to your own world."

"Not until I see Lilja and determine that she's all right." He didn't trust the old man. Apparently, they still hadn't discovered the lake portal. He sure wasn't giving it away.

"Have Lilja join us," said the light-haired elder.

"No doubt she is dancing by the firelight," Lukais said dismissively.

"If she has an attachment to this human, I doubt she will mind missing the dancing this one night," returned the other man.

"I will send for her and see if she is willing to participate," said Lukais. "I cannot, of course, make her attend."

"He's stalling," Grey said flatly. "Lilja will come if she knows I'm here, unless he's got her locked up. Let her come so we can all see she's okay." He worried at the stall tactics. Had she been harmed? Sweat trickled down between his shoulder blades. "If you've hurt her," he said harshly, "there won't be a faerie realm big enough for you to hide."

***

Lilja crouched in the dark, panicked by the unfamiliar sounds and smells of this place. The damp and musty realm of the Deevs invaded her nostrils and pressed heavily on her chest. Beneath her, the ground clung with sticky persistence to her hands and feet. When she'd fallen into this dark place, she'd tried to stand, but the space only allowed her to crouch or sit.

Lukais' magic had sucked her to this lonely exile, a timeless place where she remained uncertain if it was night-time or if it was a place of perpetual darkness.

Several times something touched her leg and then her arm, and she'd swatted it away. The longer she remained, the more she felt panic closing in on her. She had never heard of Aisywel faeries being sent to the Deevs realm. All she knew were stories passed down through time of their evil inclinations.

She heard a whirring and felt something breathing close beside her. Her heart had never beat so hard in her chest. She bit her lips to keep from crying out as she felt a pinch on her calf. She swatted it away and then felt something bite one of her toes. With a strangled cry, she backed up. Was she to be eaten alive then, bit by bit?

Something solid was at her back. Her hands felt the rough surface, and realized she was in some kind of corner. She wrapped her arms tightly around herself. When she sensed the creature move close to her again, it touched her foot. She pushed it away.

"Leave me alone," she said into the dark. "I didn't come here to harm anyone."

"A sweet little faerie?" asked a raspy voice almost in her ear. "The most delicious kind." Lilja tried to pull back but there was nowhere to go. "What must you have done," continued the voice, "that you would be sent here for our sport?"

"I have done nothing," Lilja said -- except that she had defied Lukais. Lilja worried about Grey. If Lukais would do this to a faerie, what would he do to a human? She bit her lips. First Pandimora, then Peri -- now Grey. He was taking away everyone she cared about.

"The elder sends us those who have done the faerie realm a grave injustice."

Lilja began to shake as cool air brushed over and around her and a pinpoint of light suddenly began to appear in front of her. She kept her gaze fixed on that light, but then realized it came from somewhere above her.

"If you feared the night, now comes the day," said the voice.

Light began to fill in the space around her, allowing her to see what the dark had hidden. She was at the bottom of a cavern, under a lip of stone which was preventing her from standing. She moved out from under the jutting rock, and now the light from above shone directly on her. Quickly, she turned her head to see a creature no bigger than her palm hovering in front of her face.

It appeared to be female, with rapidly moving gossamer wings that she could barely see. The face had large deep-set black eyes, a garish red slash of a mouth and fangs that overlapped its thin lips. It had no nostrils.

"You bit me," Lilja said.

"Of course," the creature responded. "I am always hungry, never satisfied. You are a fresh soul to nourish my hungry body."

"I'm not here by choice," Lilja protested.

"No soul chooses to fall here," was the response, "but fall they do."

Lilja shuddered. The winged creature flitted away and hovered about ten feet from her on a small shelf-like rock. It watched her, as if savoring its next meal.

"I don't belong here, you know," she said quietly.

"None of them do," came the whisper.

"There are others?"

"Some." It tilted its head. "Why aren't you afraid? The live ones always are."

"I'm afraid, but I'm not going to plead with you. No living creature is allowed to consume a live soul."

The creature opened its mouth and cackled. The sound ran a shiver down Lilja's back.

"An Aisywel faerie is the freshest soul imaginable. A rare delicacy."

Lilja put her hand up as the creature was suddenly a hair's breadth from her face, its mouth open. Terrified, Lilja stared at the sharp teeth, which now looked incredibly large. She swatted it as hard as she could but that seemed to only make it angry.

Vaguely, she heard a soft thunk and the creature dropped to the stone floor. Lilja jumped in terror to the other side of the cavern, staring as a light green mist encircled the dead creature and it slowly disintegrated.

"Up here," said a deep male voice.

With a screech, Lilja looked up. At the top of the tunnel, shadowed by the light behind him, stood a man with a slingshot.

Was she to be stoned as the creature had been?

"You don't have to commit a crime to be here," said the man's voice. "And have no fear, I'm not going to stone you," he said.

"You're reading my mind."

There was impatience in his voice. "You'll have to crawl out. Do you see the passage?"

She looked around and saw a small opening under the outcropping of rock where the creature had sat and watched her. She swallowed. It was very small.

"Yes, it is small," he called down, "but you can get through. Daylight is almost over. It will be twilight when you get to the end, but I'll be waiting for you."

Lilja swallowed. Daylight had just broken and now darkness so soon? How long was the tiny passage? Could she trust him?

"Who else will you trust?" his voice came down to her. Looking up, she saw he was gone.

Biting her lips, she put a hand into the dark hole and felt only cool air. What choice did she have -- stay in this hole in the ground? She closed her eyes, concentrating on making herself smaller, but her magic did not work in this world. She knelt, ducked her head and pushed her shoulders against the stone. It gave way and slowly she crawled into the small space.

"You're almost there," the same male voice sounded almost in her ear.

"I just began." Relieved, she stifled a cry as strong hands pulled her from the hole into near dark. A shadowy figure helped her stand upright. He was very tall, even taller than Grey.

"We have to move quickly." He gripped her hand.

"There will be others. I can hold them off only so long."

"Other Deevs?" she asked.

He gave a sharp laugh and Lilja stumbled along behind him as he pulled her with him.

"Deevs indeed. All the faeries swallow so blandly what they are told," he declared, his voice now angry and passionate.

"What do you mean?"

"You're being fed lies," he said, still moving quickly in the near dark, the ground uneven beneath their feet. "As Aisywel is a lie."

"You're a faerie," she said slowly. "What is this place?"

"Dinorma," he said flatly. "A place even a Deevs will not go."

Terror seeped into her. *Land of the lost.*

"I'm taking you to the way back," he said, his voice now reassuring, as if he understood everything she felt.

"There's a way back?" Lilja felt a ray of hope in this dark world.

"There's always a way back."

"Who are you?" Lilja asked.

"It doesn't matter."

"It does to me."

"Here in this cursed place, I am merely a survivor. Hold on to me." He gripped her strongly around the waist and Lilja's feet left the ground. She felt as if they were swinging through the air. Terrified again, she held on as tightly as she could.

"Put your feet down when I say so. Now!"

She stiffened her knees and they touched the

ground with a slight jolt. His arm kept her from falling, then once she was steady, he left her side.

At her feet Lilja began to see a faint green mist. The same mist that had engulfed the dead creature.

"Don't be afraid," he said. "This light will take you back."

She turned toward him. "Come with me," she urged. "You don't belong here." She tried to see him in the swirling mist, but all she saw was his shadowed outline. Strong jaw, long hair, and as he turned from her she saw his arm was marked by powerful Celtic symbols.

"I'm cursed to live out my life here," he said harshly. "You must leave before you are tainted by the atmosphere and your fate becomes the same. Envision where you wish to go."

"Tell me the name of the faerie who saved me!"

"Kirklas."

He pushed her into the soft glow as it rose up in front of her.

"I am Lilja ..." She would never know if her voice reached him.

***

Grey couldn't believe the council was blind to Lukais' tactics. The old man strode about as if he had all the time in the world. Patiently, the elders listened.

"Lukais, what is this human's offense?" said the light-haired elder.

The old man turned fierce eyes on him. "You question my wisdom?"

"We sense no threat from him," the black haired elder said patiently. "We wish him to see we are reasonable and wish him no harm, so release him."

"My name is Grey." Grey watched Lukais warily. Immobilized as he was, he wouldn't be able to defend himself if the old man tried something.

Lukais faced his peers. "As elders, we are responsible for the safety of all in the faerie realm. Lilja has chosen to visit the human world more and more and has allowed this human to bewitch her to the point where she believes she will be better off in their world than her own." He turned to face Grey and the anger on his face and in his eyes seemed almost spiteful. "She has allowed this human to touch her."

"Release him." The black-haired elder's voice rose, as if suddenly out of patience.

With a sound of disgust, Lukais waved his hand.

Instantly, Grey could move. He stood, rubbing his wrists. It felt as if steel handcuffs had held him in place. His chair moved behind him, puddled to the floor and transformed into a large green snake. Grey stepped back quickly, but the snake gave him a bored look from its slitted dark eyes and slithered away. Grey stared after it. How did that snake manage to convey its boredom? He kept an eye on the snake until it exited the glass dome.

The light-haired elder nodded his head. "Please allow me to introduce myself. I am Bernate."

"And I am Matlei," said the black-haired elder.

Grey looked at Lukais, but the old man ignored him.

He addressed Bernate and Matlei. "It's true Lilja came to my world. She has a tremendous gift for healing, and she healed my sick animals."

"And you would take her from us," Lukais said angrily. "Lilja has always shown great promise in Aisywel."

"Surely it's her choice to stay or go?" Grey stared at Lukais. "I wonder, though, why you're so angry. From what I understand faeries have been visiting with humans for centuries. You even created portals so you could come and go as you wish into our world. It's not the humans who initiated the contact."

"How do we know other humans won't follow you here?" Lukais turned away from Grey and appealed to Bernate and Matlei. "This human carries weapons in his world and imprisons his own kind."

"I am an officer of the law," Grey said. "If you've studied our world, you know it's a part of our system to maintain law and order." Impatiently, he said, "Listen, enough of this stalling. Make him tell you what he's done with Lilja."

"Grey!" Lilja's voice was suddenly behind him. Grey spun around and was shocked by her filthy and bedraggled appearance. Her hands were stained with a black substance and her light colored dress had black and green stains all over it.

"Lukais! Tell the council how you maintain order in Aisywel," she said. "You send faeries to Dinorma!"

Grey didn't know what Dinorma was but based on her appearance and Lukais' angry denial, it wasn't good. As Grey strode toward Lilja, all chaos broke loose.

He didn't trust Lukais and knew he had to reach her first. Grey dove toward her on the smooth floor, vaguely aware of blue light snapping like live wires, the light almost blinding as it bounced off the glass around them. Rolling to his feet, he grabbed her and took both of them down to the floor.

Snakes of light from Lukais' wooden stick hit Bernate and Matlei. They dropped to the glass table, out cold. Then, airborne and coming fast, Lukais swung around, pointing his stick at Grey and Lilja. Grey figured it would be similar to lightning and would kill them both. He tried to shield her but Lilja pushed him back so he skittered away from her on his back.

Lilja flung out her hand and seemed to catch the light that Lukais shot at her. Her body jerked and then she went stiff. Grey tried to get to her, but in the span of microseconds, light traveled from her palm, up her arm and stopped at her shoulder. Through the material of her dress, he could see the spiral tattoo turn bright red and then gold as it burned away the flimsy fabric of her garment.

Grey heard glass splintering and wondered if the entire place would fall around their heads, burying them in deadly shards. He was amazed when Lukais stumbled back as an incredible force of light three times the size of the one he'd directed at them now shot at him from Lilja's palm. Grey had only a second to see the shock in Lukais' eyes before it rocked the old man off his feet and slammed him against the glass wall. He slid down the wall to the ground and lay writhing.

Looking shaken, Lilja turned to him. "Grey, are you all right?"

"Me?" he said harshly, finally reaching her. "What did he do to you?"

She leaned against him a moment, her body trembling. "I don't know, but somehow I was able to send the energy back to him. We must act quickly," she said. "He will soon rally."

"That electric jolt would have killed anyone else," Grey muttered. Bernate and Matlei were still passed out on the table. No help there. Lilja grabbed the stick Lukais had dropped. She approached the old man with the stick out before her.

Slowly, two incredibly beautiful crystals levitated out of his robe. They hovered in the air a moment then swiftly moved toward Lilja. She caught them in one hand, a beautiful emerald green crystal and a clear one, both about three inches long and the width of a cigar.

"Now we are on common ground," Lilja said, carefully placing the crystals within an inner pocket.

Rolling onto his back, Lukais began to laugh weakly. "The irony. The pupil has become the aggressor."

"You began this fight," she said, pushing the glowing stick against Lukais' chest. Grey shielded his eyes from the glow as bright as a welder's torch.

"As I escaped Dinorma," she said, "I remembered the family you took from me. What have you done to them?"

Grey clamped his mouth shut. He needed to tell her about Pandimora as soon as he could, but not in front of Lukais.

"I am not their keeper," snapped Lukais.

Lilja pressed harder and the torch changed to a blue flamed ball.

Grey felt the heat of the flame four feet away and

kept his eyes averted.

"I don't know," Lukais finally gasped. "They may be scattered to the four corners. Only you, my dear Lilja, were valuable enough to keep here in Aisywel. If only you had remained cooperative, we could have had all worlds at our feet."

Lilja appeared unmoved by his words. "Where is Peri?" she demanded.

"Remember the faerie rhyme?" And he smiled. "What was up now is down until the grass is the sky and the sky is no more."

Grey wanted to smash his sly, insolent face.

Suddenly a translucent red film began to envelope Lukais. His eyes rolled back in his head as he tried to regain his feet, but then his legs straightened and his arms went to his sides. His eyes closed. He looked as if he'd been laid out for burial. That suited Grey just fine, but Lilja still had no answers.

"Lukais has been enclosed in a suspended state," said Bernate, coming up behind them.

Grey saw that the elder now held the two crystals Lilja had taken from Lukais.

"How could this happen?" Grey asked. "Lilja told me Aisywel was supposed to be a beautiful place full of joy. How could he have pulled off this con for so long?"

Matlei held his head stiffly erect. "You are correct to condemn our blindness. Lukais will go before the tribunal and his actions through all time will be examined. We will discover why he turned against the faerie."

"And meanwhile Lilja's questions go

unanswered," Grey said, staring at the tired, dirty face of the woman he loved. "Her family is missing." He took her chin and brought her gaze to his. "I can tell you, though, I know your sister is safe," he said. "I can tell you that at least." The hope in her eyes was encouraging to see. She threw her arms around his neck.

"Grey! You know where my sister is?"

He nodded. "She's safe with my brother Drew."

Bernate looked at Lukais. "It was understood that Pandimora left of her own free will."

"I spoke to her," Grey said. He looked at Lilja. "She is in my world now -- the earth. She saw Lukais strike down another faerie and that discovery put her in danger."

Lilja clasped her hands. "She is safe!"

"She escaped and arrived on the earth realm mortally wounded," Drew said quietly. "She's unable to return to Aisywel due to Lukais' banishing her." He turned to the elder. "Lilja's friend Peripaus has also vanished, and all she did was try to help."

Lilja looked at Lukais lying so serenely before them. "He banished my entire family and my dearest friend."

"Pandimora told me her memories were erased, but with the help of the Aisywel crystals, she was able to access some of the past. Your mother Clare marked both of you for protection."

Matlei, looking distressed, put a hand to his forehead. "This is horrific. It must all be sorted out. Pandimora must return and give witness."

Grey shook his head. "How can her safety be assured? She told me she bargained with goblins to get back into Aisywel to not only find her sister, but to warn the high elder council. I think you will have to go to her."

Lilja pressed her fingertips to her temples. "The memories are still clouded."

Drew reached for her hand. "Pandimora suspects Lukais had something to do with your parents' disappearance from Aisywel." His attention went back to the crystals in the elder's hand. Sparks seemed to bounce off their facets, hitting the glass walls all around them and creating brilliant light.

Lilja said, "All this time I was misled. I trusted his wisdom."

"You're more than a match for him," Grey said quietly, impressed with how she'd conducted herself. A woman of lesser integrity might have killed him while she had the opportunity for the way he'd wronged her family.

Bernate looked at Lilja. "There were concerns -- but it appears we have all been duped. Lilja, you were sent to Dinorma -- and yet here you are. How did you manage to escape Dinorma?"

"I had help. I'm certain he was a faerie. I asked him to come with me, but he said he was cursed and couldn't leave." She put a hand to her mouth. "He saved me from being consumed by a voracious creature."

"Geez, Lilja." Grey turned to the elder. "She's lucky to have survived."

"Only dead souls descend to that dimension," Matlei said slowly. "I am not aware of any way in or out for a live being. It is a dimension created in ancient times. I fear our entire realm may be askew from Lukais's manipulations."

Bernate said, "Lilja, tell us what you know."

"Lukais washed my mind of memories of my sister. As I passed from Dinorma I remembered my family from when I was an infant. A bare speck of time, my parents, my brother and sister, before they all disappeared." She took the hand Grey held out to her. "Lukais sent me there for defying him, and perhaps he intended to leave me there."

Matlei regarded her steadily. "These are grave accusations," he cautioned.

"And what about what happened here today?" Grey said impatiently.

She lifted her chin. "I stand by my accusation."

"There is something else Pandimora asked me to convey," Grey said gravely. "As we speak the Deevs flood the southern corners of Aisywel."

"We have been puzzling how such an event occurred," said Bernate. "We had begun negotiations with the Deevs, but talks broke off when Lukais refused to listen to their demands."

It wasn't reassuring to Grey that the elders looked very worried.

With furrowed brow, Matlei said to Grey, "An investigation must be conducted immediately. The portals will be unsealed but it may take a little time. The crystal power must be transferred carefully and completely from Lukais' control and he will be rigorously questioned before a tribunal.

"There is much we need to discuss before a ruling can be made." He looked at Lilja and gently took her hand. "We will send for you when a determination has been made as to Lukais' fate. It is a sad time when such havoc is wreaked upon gentle Aisywel."

∞ Chapter Eleven ∞

Lilja held Grey's hand tightly as they walked outside into the balmy night air. Pressing a hand to her heart, she looked up at Grey's dear face. "My heart is full and yet I feel pain. I'm heartsick over what I've learned and what I still don't know. And how did you arrive here, Grey -- traversing the worlds to find me? It could have turned out disastrously for you."

"Pandimora helped me get here using the lake portal since she couldn't cross into Aisywel. I've been out of my mind with worry since he took you. Dinorma sounds like a nightmare come to life."

A shiver shook Lilja's frame. "Explain a nightmare."

"A dream that is incredibly frightening, one you feel like you can't escape, and everything in it scares the heck out of you."

She nodded. "That is an apt description." And

Lilja told him of her experience in the dark twilight of Dinorma. "If it had not been for that man, I might have perished there. I wish there was a way to free him from that place. I sensed he didn't belong."

Grey pulled her closer. "I'm sorry I wasn't there to protect you when the elder forced you away."

Lilja touched his cheek. "Grey, you would have been powerless against him, and he would have certainly hurt you if you'd gotten in his way."

"Is he really immobile and powerless now?"

Lilja worried her lip with her teeth. "I hope so."

"Yeah, I'm a bit skeptical also."

Lilja clasped her hands. "When they release the portals from Lukais' power, we can leave. But for now, please tell me what you know. I hope hearing about Pandimora will release my memories."

He looked at the green light rolling along the ground like mist. He couldn't help it; this place raised the hair on the back of his neck. "Pandimora is just as anxious to see you. Can we go back to your cottage and talk?"

"Yes. I will be glad to relax in my dear little cottage."

Lilja took Grey's large calloused hand in her own and led him toward a glimmering portal suspended in air. They stepped through it. To Grey it looked like hundreds of tiny lights. He looked back as the portal disappeared and they entered her cottage.

"No offense, sweetheart, but I don't think I'll ever get used walking two steps into an entirely different area." Her cottage was still softly lit. "Your sister gave me explicit directions how to find your cottage so I came here first. I kept hearing voices," he added, keeping his voice low.

"My plants always greet visitors," she said, tenderly touching the flowers over the door, then running her hand over tree limbs which had been shaped into a chair. "They do the same in your world, Grey."

He lifted a brow. "I don't hear them," he said.

She moved over to the porcelain bowl. Water flowed from a spout and she began to wash the marks of Dinorma from her hands and arms.

Grey moved up behind her, wrapping his arms around her waist, then splaying his fingers across her stomach. Lilja closed her eyes, sinking back against him, loving the protective quality that Grey projected.

"I don't see any plumbing or pipes," he murmured.

"It's not necessary," Lilja said, tilting her head so his lips could touch her skin. "The water comes from nature and flows freely to wherever I need it."

She dried her face and hands with a small hand towel. When she let go of the towel, it turned into white butterflies that fluttered around the room and then out a small crack in the window casing.

"My sister came to your ranch? How does she look? Is she well?"

"I think she's been through an ordeal, my brother also. She was mind washed, Lilja, just as you were, but she was mind washed twice, once as a child the night your family disappeared and again when she saw the elder strike down another faerie."

Lilja covered her mouth with her hands.

"All this time, she's been trying to get back here

to find you. From what Drew said, she almost died. I think they've saved each other a few times, but we'll have to get the full story when we return. It sounds complicated."

"Now I understand why I kept thinking of Pandimora but I couldn't bring up any memories. And I have other family," she added, frowning. "Perhaps the elders will be able to obtain the information from Lukais." She shook her head, sad for all the heartbeats of time she had thought him a caring faerie. "It's so distressing to find out the truth about Lukais. He's been a powerful force in our world for a long time."

"Perhaps too long," Grey murmured.

Lilja nodded. "Do I look like my sister?" she asked.

Grey laughed softly. "You both look distinctly different," he admitted. "Pandimora has flame red hair but I'm particular to dark hair with deep pink highlights myself."

Lilja materialized a bed in one corner of the room. "I would like to refresh myself with a nap, how about you, Grey?" Lilja in truth felt exhausted. The bed she'd created was large enough to accommodate Grey, and it looked very inviting.. Feathery ferns peeked out from under the pale green sheets with its soft downy comforter. She saw him looking dubiously at the delicate piece of furniture.

"I'd hate to break it," he said.

Lilja slowly turned, and as she did so she discarded the dirty dress. Standing naked before Grey, she looped her arms around his neck. "The bed will adjust to our combined weight."

"You're beautiful," he said, his hands gently resting on either side of her hips, fingertips caressing her skin. Lilja caught her breath, already seeing delicate strings of light playing between their bodies.

"Now that I am clean," she said with a gentle smile.

He grinned. "You're always beautiful to me." He leaned down to her, kissing the sensitive skin below her ear. "However, I think this is one of the rare times I haven't seen you laughing."

"I know, Grey. I am feeling the weight of all that has occurred." She sank gracefully to the bed. The sheets and comforter embraced her and she extended her hand entreatingly to Grey.

Grey crossed his arms and pulled his T-shirt over his head. Lilja stared at the smoothly sculpted muscle of his arms, his naked chest, the dusting of hair as he joined her.

"Faeries don't have such lovely muscles," she remarked, eagerly pressing kisses to his bare chest.

Gingerly, Grey rolled over to lie on his back, pulling her half on top of him. "You'll have to excuse my caution," he said gruffly. "I'm still remembering a chair that turned into a snake."

"I know, and for that I am sorry. You must find my world very strange, Grey." She waved her hand to indicate the cottage. "All that you see here are vibrant organisms that live with me in cooperation and mutual respect. If I leave this place, they will all go on with their lives elsewhere in the realm. They honor me by coming together to provide a lovely little cottage." Lilja brushed her hair from her eyes. "I am thankful you found your way without being trapped by the dusk faeries."

"Your sister gave me detailed instructions."

Lilja closed her eyes, her brow furrowed in concentration. She gripped his hands. "How could I have forgotten my sister?"

"At this point I would say you've suffered a lot of stress. Let's give it time. The elder really mistreated both of you."

Lilja shivered. "How did it happen that Pandimora is with your brother?"

"She was critically injured and somehow ended up on earth. My brother Drew eventually got her to a healing sanctuary, but he ended up going through the portal with her."

"And all this time she's been looking for me." Lilja placed her palm over her heart. "Grey, I would like something vibrant and alive so I can forget the turmoil and pain that still permeates me. I need your help."

"Anything, sweetheart."

"Make love with me," she whispered, "here in my little cottage where the energy is clear and without impedance."

He lifted a brow.

"If you're exhausted --"

She put a finger to his lips, and he kissed it. "If we create enough energy between us, we will exhaust each other," she said with a return of her impish smile.

She undid the snap of his jeans, gently placing her warm palms against his skin under the waistband. She felt his body tense, then he lifted his hips and pushed the jeans down his legs.

Lilja closed her eyes, letting her lips feel their way across his body. Such a man who braved the faerie world to find her, a man whose heart was no longer fractured. A man she could love forever.

***

Grey felt everything around him whirling, as if this world revolved around just him and Lilja. He'd thought the light display and charged atmosphere had been incredible the first time they'd made love, but now as they joined their bodies, the intensity of emotion and physical sensation was almost overwhelming. As he sank into her warm embrace, his body joining with hers, everything around them vibrated gently. She sat atop him, sinking down onto his body, and he tried to keep the pace slow even as his mind was ready to go into overload. She moved with excruciating slowness, the glide of skin on skin almost more than he could bear.

Grey tenderly cupped her breasts, just the right size, loving them and as she moved above him. He kissed her pert nipple, tracing around each one with his tongue, feeling the catch of her breath. She squeezed her legs around him and he felt as if he was skyrocketing out into space. Sensation zeroed in on the two of them where their skin touched, thin blue currents snapping between them.

He felt what she felt, her experience as he moved inside her body, and it doubled his own pleasure, giving him intricate knowledge how to thrust, what she liked, what felt the best, what brought her close to total loss of control.

They played a game with each other, each one bringing the other close to that ultimate falling-off-the-edge-of-the-earth feeling, then slowing the pace. Tenderly he cupped her cheeks to kiss her mouth. Her tongue ran over his teeth and then delved into his mouth.

She pulled away from him, lying on her back, and Grey followed her, kissing his way down her body, her skin fragrant with her unique scent. He traced her navel, delved inside a moment, felt her quiver, then he moved lower, gently parting her legs, kissing her slowly, touching her with the tip of his tongue, looking up the length of her body, her back arched off the bed, her body tight as a bowstring and vibrating. They had all the time in the world to discover each other, but now they needed to bring each other the ultimate pleasure.

Surging upwards, Drew slid into her welcoming body, letting her set the pace as they moved in unison. The electricity in the air around them felt incredible; shards of light hit them and bounced off the walls.

Lilja gripped Grey's buttocks, arching her back even more as he came into her once again. And then it all began to unravel. Any sense of control was lost as they tumbled over the edge, the orgasm hitting them hard and fast, and Grey was certain he spun past control and out to space, feeling as if everything inside shattered and blew him apart.

***

While the faeries still slept, Lilja showed Grey the true beauty of Aisywel. She took him to see the beautiful silver lake with the early morning mists hovering over its placid surface, and introduced him to the glowing meadow as the sun's first light began to creep across hillock and dale. They walked under the mystical ancient trees with their roots deeply embedded in Aisywel's rich black soil, enjoying fractured golden light as the sun's rays seeped through the trees sheltering limbs.

"Grey, I want to share with you all that Aisywel means to me."

"I can see it's a special place," he said. "It's one of unmatched beauty."

She nodded, but her expression was troubled. "Yes, but even now I feel a certain change, an element of fear I've never experienced before. Our world is changing, and I am not sure whether it is for the good or not."

"Are you afraid of the Deevs coming in?"

"They are here already," she said. "Hiding. I am not afraid of change, I just wish there was an easier way to implement the change rather than the anger and aggression I feel will accompany it. Aisywel faces challenging times ahead." Solemnly, she looked up at him. "I am hopeful the elder council will uncover what truths they can from Lukais, but he has a will of iron. I ache to think of these peaceful grounds becoming a place of struggle."

"I'd like you to come home with me, Lilja, so that we can make a life together. Please think about it."

"I'd love to live between both worlds, Grey. I hope it will be possible. Right now I am anxious to see my sister and find out what she knows about our family."

"I'll help however I can. I'm pretty sure my

brother is committed to helping also." He hesitated, then added, "Your sister did say your mother was a powerful white witch. Before she disappeared, she marked each of you for protection." Grey touched the symbol on her shoulder. "I think that's what we saw happen when the elder attacked. The way you fought against him was amazing."

"I've never had such an experience, Grey. I felt as if all the power of Aisywel was behind me, helping me." She shook her head sadly. "He was my mentor since I was a child; the teachings, the gentle laughter -- it all meant nothing."

"Perhaps when he was your mentor it was genuine, Lilja."

"But something twisted everything around. I may never know why."

Lilja tilted her head, listening. She turned to find the elder Bernate approaching them. He bowed in greeting.

"Lilja, Grey. Please understand Lukais' actions have shaken us, and already terrible repercussions are being felt in the realm and throughout the worlds. The powers he held for a thousand years as an elder have been sorely abused. We have not been able to draw out the information we hoped to regarding your parents or your brother."

Lilja drew in a sharp breath. "And Peri?" she asked barely above a whisper.

"Peripaus was placed under a spell of enchantment. Lukais intended to send her to a neighboring faerie realm, but something went amiss." He shook his head. "We do know that Peripaus was in transition when she was rerouted.

However, we have not yet discovered her whereabouts."

Lilja shook her head with despair. "Faeries can disappear like wisps of dust," she said. "Peri is very smart and quick. She must have escaped!"

Bernate bowed his head. "There are no words to express our regret over this abuse. The council is in part responsible. Lukais is being transported to the lowest vibrational plane and will be held there one thousand years and ten."

"Dinorma?" Lilja whispered, hardly daring to say it aloud.

"Yes." He bowed to both of them, stepped back and disappeared.

Numbly, she turned to Grey. Her thoughts were squeezed into a painful cold ball. "He has taken away a family I could have loved," she said. "And I don't even know why."

***

Grey watched Lilja sleep, curled up in his arms as they lay in her fern bed. The feathery ferns seemed to almost cradle her, swaying gently against her, as if soothing her to sleep. This world was so strange to him, and yet he actually felt the care the plants extended to Lilja. He itched to get back to his own world, but he knew that it was important that Lilja be able to stay here until she was ready to leave.

He saw again her bedraggled appearance in the glass dome hall, the bites on her feet and legs. It tore at him to see her so dispirited, she who from the moment he'd met her exuded energy and light and happiness. He didn't know what to do other than offer what comfort he could as she absorbed the implications of Lukais tearing her family apart. Grey couldn't imagine being separated from his family, and the pain she must be feeling ripped at him.

Lilja turned within his arms, pressing her fingers to her forehead, opening her eyes and gazing at him, her beautiful bluish-green eyes drawing him in until he wanted to drown in them.

He loved her.

She suddenly bolted upright, her eyes wide in alarm. "Grey -- your horses -- here in the faerie realm time is different from your world."

"How much different?" he asked, not having thought of that.

"Time moves very rapidly in your world, while here it is measured by heartbeats."

"Sweetheart, you're going to have to translate that for me," he said.

"Grey, while you have been here what might feel like only a day, in your time several days or weeks could have elapsed."

"My brother Drew is standing by. We'll go when you're ready."

She bowed her head. "I admit I am afraid."

"Why, sweetheart?"

"I can't remember my sister. A deep guilt swells deep inside me. What if I return to the earth realm and I still don't remember her? After all, she risked her life to find me." She sighed. "There is no need to linger and you must return to assure your family you are well. I love Aisywel, but now it feels as if it is crumbling around me."

"Maybe in time you'll see things differently."

She shivered. "I already have." Decisively, she

stood. "I am ready to leave." She looked at him. "Together?"

Grey nodded. "Always. You've been so strong, so determined to defend those you care about. I wish there had been a better resolution for you."

Lilja laid her hand on his arm. "Even as a child, you were a caring soul, Grey. I love that about you."

She grabbed his hand and pulled him toward the window at the back of the cottage. He watched curiously as she touched the glass and her hand disappeared into it.

"Another portal?" he asked.

"Yes." Lilja linked her arm with his.

"Where will it take us?"

She smiled. "Anywhere we wish to go." The glass dissolved in front of them and then around them. Lilja's sweet pure voice rose as she began to sing. It pulled at something deep inside Grey, and he knew he had to have her in his life permanently. She'd become too important to him in the time he had known her for him to let her go.

It was like stepping through a doorway; he looked behind them and saw the cottage and everything inside had dissolved back to nature; looking ahead, he saw they were back at his land, the cabin and barns in the distance.

They had stepped through the portal ... into spring-time.

***

Pandimora stood in Grey's kitchen and paused to listen. Her heart beat faster as an old Celtic faerie song wound around her, softly at first and then growing stronger. The sweet scent of lavender drifted on the spring air through the open screen door, bringing with it strong stirrings of the place she used to call home, *Aisywel*.

With legs trembling, she pushed the screen door open, stepped out onto the front porch. Looking out over the field, she looked past the horses as they kicked up their feet across the new spring grass. She caught her breath.

"Drew!" she called. "Drew!" She moved down the steps and she began to run.

Drew came running from the direction of the barns and Pandimora bit her lips, her throat tight as she pointed toward the field.

"Go," he said.

She began to run faster, tears streaming down her cheeks as she ran to meet her sister, whose hand was entwined with Grey's.

The faerie song of healing wound all around Pandimora and the tears flowed faster as she finally embraced the sister she had thought lost to her.

***

Lilja's heart overflowed with joy and her voice stilled as she embraced her sister.

She clung tightly to her, not willing to let go for many long moments.

"How could we have been separated?" she finally cried. "How did I forget? We were told you left our world of your own accord, and yet no one knew where you had gone or even spoke of you." Lilja hugged her sister again. "Pandimora, all this time I've had a spell of forgetfulness. I no longer knew I had a sister."

"It does not matter," Pandimora said, tears

shining on her cheeks. "It is over." She looked at Drew. "Somehow, the memories became untangled when he brought me here to his world."

"And you fell in love," Lilja said, delighted, clapping her hands. "Our time apart has been filled with many traumatic events, and yet it has also been full of wonder. My sister is brought home to me." Lilja gently touched her sister's cheek. "A new beginning is always great cause for celebration," she added.

"Lilja," Grey said, "this is my brother Drew, as you probably already know. Drew, my light, Lilja."

"I'm happy to meet you Lilja," Drew said, looking very much like Grey except for his lighter hair. "Thank God you've both returned safely. Pandimora's been beside herself with worry."

Pandimora lifted a brow. "And I was the only one who paced and fretted?"

"How long was I gone?" Grey asked.

"Almost three weeks. I told your boss we had a family emergency." Drew stared at his brother, as if there were things that needed to be discussed. "Mom and Dad weren't so easily put off."

Lilja clasped Grey's hand to her heart, her eyes softened with love and gratitude. "Grey is a brave man to come after me."

Grey lifted a brow. "And she ended up rescuing me," he admitted ruefully. "Though if I had magic, the playing field might have been leveled out."

Pandimora smiled. "Perhaps. But then in the faerie realm things are not always as they appear."

At Grey's puzzled expression, she continued, "When a human enters the faerie realm, everything the human experiences is an illusion."

Lilja nodded. "We resize based upon your perceived notion of faeries."

Grey lifted a brow. "Really?"

"While in Aisywel, faeries are really no bigger than a six-year-old human child," Lilja said.

Grey laughed, but a touch of color rose in his cheeks. "So I was held captive by a council no larger than six-year-olds." He narrowed his eyes. "And what about my chair that turned into a snake?"

"That was very real," Lilja said. "You might have been a threat, so they were wary and troubled by your presence."

She turned back to her sister.

"Pandimora, there is so much we need to speak about. My hope is that one day we will stand together with our complete family." She looked out across the hills, her mouth trembling. "And I hope I can discover the whereabouts of my dear friend Peri."

Pandimora's eyes widened in shock. "Peri is missing?"

Lilja nodded. "Perhaps someday we will return to Aisywel," she said sadly. "When it is restored to what it was."

Pandimora shook her head. "Any fond memories have been erased for me. I fear nothing ever goes back the way it was." Pandimora gave her a worried frown. "More and more faeries are integrating into this world. Soon, there will be no more Aisywel. There is much Lukais has to answer for," her sister added in a hard voice.

"Lukais has been transported to Dinorma."

Pandimora looked concerned. "I hope Dinorma will hold him. At this time I am less than hopeful for a resolution or answers."

"I don't know anything about our parents or our brother," Lilja said in a low voice.

"The memory washing is quite effective," Pandimora said. "You were newly born when our parents disappeared. Clare, our mother, was a human witch. Declan, our father, was high lord of the faeries, and of course, Kirklas was the eldest. Clare loved Kirklas as her own --"

Lilja gave a small shriek, her face white. "It cannot be -- a faerie -- his name was Kirklas -- helped me escape Dinorma."

Pandimora grabbed her arm. "Can it be?"

"His soul gift -- he read my mind."

"As a child, Kirklas protested his gift, but they melded it to him anyway. He can see the truth of the heart."

"I tried to get him to escape with me. Kirklas said he was cursed to remain in Dinorma. It is a place of hopeless souls forever chained."

***

Grey could see it was a difficult parting for both sisters, but Drew and Pandimora declined the use of his spare bedroom, and as their truck's tail-lights disappeared down the driveway, Grey urged Lilja to his side.

She stood on tiptoe, her feet still bare, and wound her arms around his neck. Her kiss was as unrestrained as her nature. Grey felt a vibrational shift in her, as if a part of her spirit had been set free.

"It feels right to be with you," he murmured against her.

Tenderly, she touched his face, rubbing the bristle on his chin.

"I know," he said ruefully, "I need a shave."

"I have fallen in love with you," she said with awe. "Perhaps I have been in love with you all this time. It is only now that I finally understand this depth of emotion that humans feel in their hearts. How it hurts and yet expands at the same time."

"It's been a long time since I've allowed myself to feel happy," he said. "But that's how I feel with you, Lilja. I love you."

"When I met a dark-haired little boy, I was enchanted by the beauty of that soul." Lilja laughed again, her joy carrying on the air around them.

"Marry me, Lilja. I'll help as best I can to find your family and your friend Peri. I'd like to thank her some day for what she did for you."

Tears moved to the edge of her lashes. "Grey, it might take years of searching."

"Years we'll be together," he said. "I'll help you adjust -- you may find observing human life and actually living that life are totally different."

"But the adventure!" she exclaimed. "A man I love and a new world to fully explore."

Grey frowned. "Pandimora said faeries give up immortality if they choose our world -- and what about your healing skills?" he asked, worried. "Will they remain with you?"

"My skills will remain as they are meant to be. Immortality -- what does it mean if it affords you only the memories of the love you once had?"

He sighed, leaning toward her and cupping her face with his hands. "Lilja, you sweep all worries away. Can life really operate like that? These are all integrated, important parts of you. I don't want you to lose any of it."

Tenderly, she laid the back of her hand along his cheek. "Perhaps the healing will take on new life here, but I am willing to keep my heart open and see where it takes me." She smiled at him. "In the meantime, there's a lot I know about happiness and joy that I am ready to share with you, Grey."

∞ Epilogue ∞

Lukais lay perfectly still, watching dark creatures with ridiculously low intelligence fighting over the last scraps of his white robes. He abhorred the rough black woolen garments they'd given him for clothing, but since it would be for a short duration only, he supposed he would endure them against his skin.

Inside his translucent gray holding container, he stared off into the twilight around him. *Dinorma*. He forced his mind to work through the heavy dimensional fog that pervaded this lowly place. If he were not careful, all his senses would dull and he would fall into the sleep of the dead.

He knew there was a way out. All he had to do was tap into the correct vibration and align with the almost imperceptible shift in this dimension's atmosphere when it occurred. He had found it hundreds of years ago; he could find it again.

The creatures of Dinorma were known for their skill in the games of war, a skill well documented in faerie history -- and he was an expert on faerie history. They had a voracious appetite. He would utilize both skills to his advantage when he left this dismal place.

As he studied them, they went about their business, not even bothering to glance his way. Well, that was certainly his preference. He could plot and scheme and decipher the calculations of his escape without interruption. And escape he would. After all, he was the highest elder of the faerie realm. They could not keep him here forever. And when he found the way out, oh, that would surely be the day of reckoning for human and faerie alike. He would never accept their so-called punishment. Aisywel was his and would once more bow at his feet.

The shift from light into dark was perfect. Since time was not measurable, all he had to do was mindshift into that ancient, never-recorded wormhole that would present itself at precisely the moment he decided. Even stripped of his magic, he would not be kept in this dismal, barren place.

Lukais closed his eyes. Relaxed, he even smiled. All they would find would be a drab gray box, empty.

As the light shifted, he readied himself for that tiny, tiny crack in the wormhole. He could feel his blood beginning to boil, his fingertips no doubt turning red. All in preparation. And in an instant of slipping beyond reality and space, he began to project his thoughts in between the light and dark. In his mind he saw where he must go.

Suddenly, a deafening crack of sound startled

him and he jerked upright, hitting hit his head on the container. Pressed against the outside of the translucent glass were two big hands on either side of a male face. In the last vestiges of light, Lukais recognized him.

"Kirklas!" Already it was too late.

Kirklas dematerialized into a fine wisp of vapor and sucked himself into the wormhole crack instead of Lukais.

"No!" shouted Lukais as the wormhole snapped shut. Furious beyond the ages, he beat the impenetrable walls of his translucent prison.

∞ *THE END* ∞

Once and Always

Memory could be gentle. At other times it left scars.

Anna Barlow had read those words this morning and somehow they felt like a reflection of her life. She stared out over her ranch's fields now, trying to shake off the cobwebs of old memories...

She had to live with her mistakes, but somehow she'd find a way out of this mess.

Heartstealer

Jacie's stomach churned as she stared at the ground two thousand feet below. What insanity made her put herself through this punishment—just to prove she wasn't washed up as a stunt woman?

"Just do it," she muttered. "You've done it thousands of times before. Get your foot out the door and jump."

Echoes From the Past

A woman, a man and a child with nothing in common but their respective troubled pasts. Three wounded souls determined to survive alone until they realize all they need to heal is each other.

On the verge of a nervous breakdown, Christie reacts by running away, emotionally and physically. Down to her last twenty dollars, she's determined to fulfill her dead sister's last wish -- to locate their sister Judith who left home twenty years before. Her quest brings her into the lives of Garrett, Judith's husband, and the emotionally fragile Hannah, Judith's daughter.

Soulmates Through Time: Book 2 Time travel series. Thrust from her own time in 1822, Elise has been separated from the man she loves for 24 years. She has adjusted to modern times, raised a daughter, and become successful in her own right. When she stumbles upon the way back, she must make the decision to step back into that time.

Will Darien still love her and will Elise be able to turn back the clock and regain the love they once shared? Does she want to turn back time?

Treasure So Rare: Book 3 Time Travel series. Captain Erik Remington has been haunted for three years by a black haired sea witch. They spent seven glorious days and nights before she vanished as mysteriously as she appeared.

In 1850, when his ship is pulled into a strange vortex, he ends up in middle ages England.

¤ ¤ ¤

Romantic Short Stories

Two Babies, a Cowboy and Sara: Short, sweet romance, 24,000 words. When Sara is appointed co-guardian of her deceased cousin's infant girls, their father Lucas is glad to accept Sara's help in caring for the twins. For Sara it's a labor of love and also a dream come true since she can't have babies of her own.

Deception

Short, sweet romance with a hint of suspense. Trey's boss is old, sick and his days are numbered; and he wants to see his missing granddaughter Katharine before he dies. Trey will do almost anything for the old man, even if it means having artist Sacha Fortune pretend to be Katharine.

But Sacha has more to lose than Trey could ever guess.

Faeries Lost Series
Find Me ~ Book 1:   Pandimora loves the faerie realm Aisywel, but she's a bit of a rebel, has little interest in the rich faerie history, loves to listen in on private conversations and hops portals into the earth realm against the advice of the high elders.

All in all her independent spirit isn't going so well in the faerie realm, but what she knows about herself as a faerie will be sorely tested when she is kicked out of Aisywel and forced to confront a terrible crime by one of her own high elders.

Hear Me ~ Book 3:   Heir to high lord of the faeries, Kirklas has managed to escape the living hell he's been exiled to for the last 10 human years. Upon his return home to Aisywel, everything is changed. Beset with civil unrest, Aisywel is in turmoil and everyone he loved is gone, and with them any hope for answers. Can he set aside the thirst for revenge or will he follow that road to its bitter end? A road that may well destroy him and the life he once hoped for.

Visit my author page at www.GraceBrannigan.com to read all my contemporary, time travel, faerie stories and short romantic stories.

Grace Brannigan